D1555453

River of Sorrows

Life History of the Maidu-Nisenan Indians

by Richard Burrill

Library of Congress Cataloging in Publication Data

Burrill, Richard, 1945—
    River of sorrows; life history of the Maidu-Nisenan Indians / by
    Richard Burrill.
        p.   cm.
    Bibliography: p.
    Includes index.
    ISBN 0-87961-186-3.   ISBN 0-87961-187-1 (pbk.) $8.95
    1. Maidu Indians—Fiction. 2 Nisenan Indians—Fiction. 3. Indians of
North America—California—Fiction. I. Title.
PS3552.U7435R5   1988
813'.54—dc19   88—25528
                                                                    CIP

Copyright © 1988 by Richard Burrill.
All rights reserved.
Printed in the U.S.A.

On the cover: *"Maidu Walk" by Maidu artist Dalbert S. Castro. Depicted is the forced march of mostly Maidu Indians in 1863 from Chico to the Round Valley Reservation in Covelo, California, 125 miles to the west. Of the 461 Indians force-marched past their sacred mountain, the Sutter Buttes, by the Second Infantry of the California Volunteers, only 277 reached the reservation, truly a "Trail of Tears" for the California Indian peoples.*

Naturegraph Publishers, Inc.
3543 Indian Creek Road
Happy Camp, CA 96039
U.S.A.

Books for a better world

I dedicate this book in memory of my loving friend H.D. "Timm" Williams, Sea Gull From The Sea, leader of his Indian people, the Yurok, and spiritual leader for all of those so fortunate, as was I, to have known him.

March 6, 1988

Acknowledgements

There are a number of people I wish to thank for their help in the completion of this book.

Norman Wilson and Arlean Towne's *Selected Bibliography of Maidu Ethnolography and Archaeology* opened the window to these Indian peoples. They, along with Dorothy Hill and Herb Puffer, gave direction to preliminary drafts.

Suggestions and help were also graciously given by Richard Simpson, Craig Bates, Brian Bibby, Lorraine Ramsdell, Louise Hendrix, Jean Nugent, Lisa Basker, my mother Martha Burrill, George Stammerjohan, Ira Heinrich, John Rumming, Harry Fonseca and Dalbert Castro. Each of these individuals, in their own way, gave me timely encouragement, otherwise this book may have never been completed in its present form.

Lastly, I owe a world of thanks to my friend, Paulette Kelley, whose "exactness to rules" rounded out the story significantly.

Foreword

Rarely in California literature can one find fictional narrative about California Indians written with the care and research that Richard Burrill has developed in *River of Sorrows*. It is a story of the Nisenan people along the American River before and after the forces of Western civilization swept across their land, destroying and changing forever their lives and the territory they knew so well.

This story developed from careful research into archeology, ethnology, and history. It is not only a study of the Nisenan during this turbulent period, but it is a sensitive story of a people: their love and hates, jealousies and celebrations. It brings to life these people who lived and died for hundreds of years before the Spanish first came to this continent.

In the study of archeology, as old village sites are excavated and information is carefully recorded about the tools, houses, and material objects, it is always frustrating to the scientist to know that the story of these people has been lost. The few physical remains of a vibrant culture tell nothing of the family, religious beliefs, or adventures and great speeches. All of us in the field of California anthropology often wonder about this great loss as we study the few remaining evidences.

The author, through his research and ability to tell a story, has brought to us an exciting pageant about a time we will never know. Most importantly, he gives us the opportunity to understand and appreciate the Nisenan, a people very much like ourselves.

Norman Wilson and Arlean Towne
(Co-authors of *Nisenan, Handbook of North American Indians*, Volume 8.)

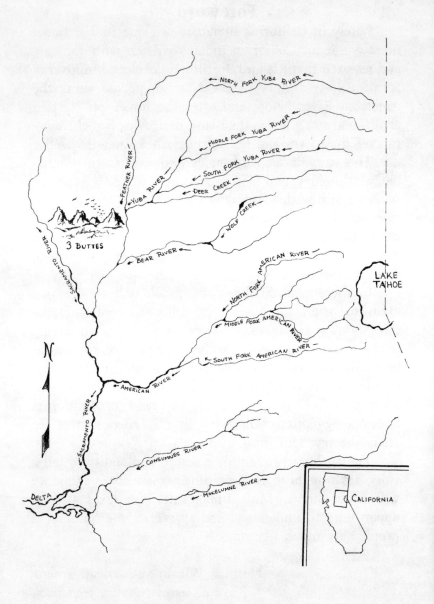

Ancestral Home of the Maidu-Nisenan
Map by Pat Darling.

Table of Contents

Prologue

There has never been an historical novel written about the beautiful Maidu-Nisenan Indians of north-central California. Few people have been willing to wade through all the anthropological documents and no one has tied together all the interesting stories into one true-to-life novel for adults and young people.

Between 1902 and 1934, Maidu and Nisenan Indians were interviewed extensively by university anthropologists such as Ralph Beals, Roland Dixon, Edward Gifford, Alfred Kroeber, C. Hart Merriam, and others. From these interviews many ethnographic articles were written. This is one author's attempt to utilize this information, as well as knowledge gleaned from resourceful Indian informants and local historians, in historical fiction, presenting the life history of the Maidu-Nisenan Indians. The appended Chapter Notes, when taken together, are testimony to the story's authenticity. Through the eyes of Tokiwa, a Nisenan medicine doctor, we witness the end of an era and feel the tragedy with Tokiwa as he experiences the destruction of his people. We watch as they adjust to a transition from their Stone Age culture to the Iron Age of the white man. This drama of day-to-day life in pre-American times sheds light upon the impact of the European-American invasion into California.

For theme, the reader participates in Tokiwa's inner struggle when he discovers he is to be a doctor for his people. Yet, Tokiwa has to resolve all the implications that go with this calling. Does he make the right choices or are events beyond his control?

As for cultural accuracy, the real Maidu-Nisenan story remains untold, especially in the areas of medicine and religion. In his contact with the Indians, John A. Sutter confessed frustrations whenever he tried to learn more about the Indian customs and culture. In his diary, Sutter concluded: "They (the Indians) dislike to impart much of such valuable information to white men. Chief Anashe's reticence is apparently due to a superstition that bad luck followed the divulgence of tribal lore." (Dillon 1967:91)

In many ways, the Maidu-Nisenan tribelets were representative of the first peoples from which we were all derived. To understand them is to see ourselves through alien eyes and thus achieve closer contact with the natural and spirit worlds. This story reveals what we have lost—the link between ourselves and the natural world. Who is the true, natural man, unfettered by the restraints of modern society? Looking inward, what ancient wisdom and significant spiritual values can we attain?

It is hoped that we who live in the present can look back at this past with empathy for those times, and feel enriched in today's world by having touched some of this past.

Richard Burrill

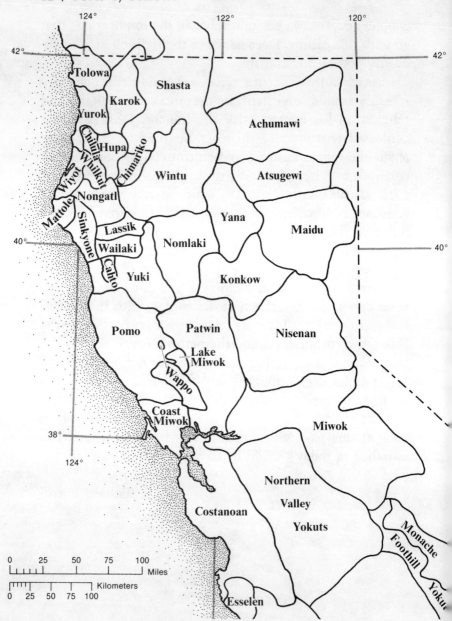

California Tribal Areas

Reprinted courtesy of Smithsonian Institution.

Introduction

A relief and population map of the greater Sacramento Valley of northern California in 1791 would reveal a lush-green, elongated valley, teeming with 76,000 California Indian people living in the midst of millions of animals and fish. The valley continued southward 300 miles, touching the San Francisco Bay delta on the west and continued south to form the San Joaquin Valley. Tule elk, grizzly bear, and wild cattle roamed across the valley floor, which was covered with grasses higher than the height of a man.

The Sacramento Valley is ringed on three sides by a great horseshoe of forested mountain ranges—the Coastal Range and jagged Trinities to the west, the Siskiyou Range to the north, and the rugged Cascade and Sierra Nevada mountain ranges to the east. Ample amounts of snow and rain tumble and rush from these mountains into the central valley, forming one main river and significant lesser rivers as well. To the Maidu-Nisenan Indian groups,* this main waterway which began on the slopes of Mount Shasta was called the Big North Water River (Sacramento River).

At the very center of this valley, as if out of nowhere, lies *Esto-Yamani,* "the middle-hills." This strange landmark, called the Sutter Buttes in historical times, and no larger than seventy-five miles square, is a holy place to the Maidu-Nisenan Indians. Their creation story taught that *Aikat,* the

---

* The Maidu Tribe divides linguistically and regionally into three distinct sub-groups: the Mountain Maidu (in the Sierras), the Konkow (the central group), and the Nisenan (the southernmost group).

Creator, kept his *Ku'-Kinim-Kumi*, spirit house, there.

Two rivers wound past these "middle-hills." To the west side meandered the Big North River deep and clear, while the sandy-bottomed *Káyimceu* (Feather River) flowed by to the east. These rivers then merged and continued south to be joined by the crystal-clear but shallow *No'to-mom* (American River), Cosumnes, and Mokelumne rivers. This water system then headed westward for 100 miles to empty into the blue Pacific Ocean.

The Valley weather was mild year round with virtually no snow. The summer days brought the "hot season" and temperatures of over 100 degrees. In the fall, the days were cool and crisp. Ground fog and intermittent rains fell through the winter (called the "ashy season") and spring—"the brush-leafing month." Ice would form on puddles at night for only a few weeks of each year. The spring brought carpets of fiery orange poppies and sky-blue lupine and more cool sun-filled days.

The Maidu-Nisenan peoples stayed within a fixed territory which included part valley and part Sierra Nevada mountains. They traded food, medicine, hides and manu-factured goods (bows and arrows and baskets) with their friendly neighbors. They, however, did not trade with the Miwok (called *Chucumnes*), whom they considered hostile.

These Indian peoples were superb at hunting, fishing and gathering, dependent in large measure on the *ooti*, or acorns, and various greens, seeds, and roots of the region. They knew the habits of each mammal and bird in detail and the identification of hundreds of species of plants.

This story begins in the white man's calendar year of 1791. There are still no white people in this part of California, only Indians. *Yamanködö* is a small Indian village on the south bank of the *No'to-mom* river. It is built on a low, natural rise with a southern exposure. One hundred and eighty Indians live in the eighteen round,

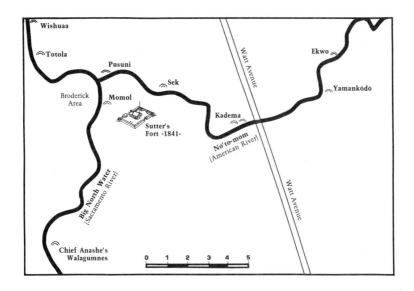

Yesterday's villages in relation to today's Watt Avenue bridge and Broderick area in Sacramento.

conically-shaped houses that cluster on the higher mound. *Yamanködö* is three miles upstream from the larger village called *Kadema** where 400 people live in forty lodges.

In several places throughout *Yamanködö* steam and smoke could be seen rising from underground cooking pits, and from tiny holes atop each of the dome-shaped lodges. Deeply tanned men, women, and children were busied with their projects, talk, and play. Two men sat together preparing fish hooks. A group of children were playing a jump dance performed to musical words, while two hunters could be seen returning to the camp along the bank of the river, each carrying over his shoulder a large haunch from a deer they had successfully hunted up river.

---

* *Kadema* village is recorded as CA-Sac-192/196.

In an adjacent pond, two women were catching fish by taking mashed soap root and stirring it in the pool until the water was soapy and foamy. This stupefied the fish which came to the surface and were easily caught in scoop baskets.

At the edge of the village, a mother was passing on to her daughter traditional basket designs, scraping willow shoots, as her daughter split sedge grass roots. Another group of women were sitting together busily cracking and hulling acorns.

Mothers strapped their babies into cradle baskets woven onto forked branches stuck vertically into the ground. As these babies viewed the world, their mothers sat on the ground with wooden mortars between their legs, raising the heavy stone pestles and letting them fall as they sang in unison. The singing of women and the synchronized thumping of a dozen pestles created a familiar sound that had continued unchanged for centuries.

The women were dressed in aprons made of the shredded inner-bark of the maple tree, with fringes dyed orange from alder bark and black from manroot berries. Two elderly women wore rabbit-skin robes while a third wore a white and grey goose-feathered cloak indicating her considerable wealth. Also the women had blue-colored tattoes that ran vertically on their chins. Some had three marks, while others five and seven.

Central to the village was the round assembly-dance house. It was the largest structure and contained few openings so that the spirits could not see inside. The interior was semi-subterranean, a four-foot-deep pit with a diameter of forty-five feet. The pit sides were lined with round logs five feet high, set on end, forming substantial walls. The low cone-shaped roof was built from radial saplings supported by two larger poles of white oak. These two main support poles, set vertically, were in a line with the ground level door that faced west. The roof was thickly covered with brush, thatch, tule, and sealed with earth.

The support pole farthest from the door was designated "spirit pole," representing the great pole that supports the world. It was honored with paints and ropes of feathers of special colors and designs. Near the spirit pole in the center of the large, earthen floor, glowed the coals of a fire set directly below the round *punkok*, or smokehole, in the roof. In this building, the Nisenan beliefs and practices were passed from one generation to another.

The deer hide door opened and a copper-colored youth entered. His hair was black and straight, and his black, deep set eyes were shining.

"Ho! Tokiwa!" called out an old brown man with a wrinkled face. "Today is a day for learning something great."

Tokiwa stood still as his eyes became accustomed to the dark inside. "What do you mean, Grandfather?" he replied politely.

"A runner came into camp while you were fishing. Headman Tawec will tell the creation story tonight in the *Kadema* dance house. I wish you to join me there."

Tokiwa nodded that he would.

He was already in his tenth year of life. Like his grandfather So-se-yah-mah, he was born along the *No'to-mom*, the "east-water" river that passed through forty Nisenan villages before it emptied into the Big North Water River at *Pusuni*, the largest and most westerly village complex on the river.

"Will the others my age be there?" Tokiwa asked.

"They have already been told," So-se-yah-mah smiled. "You need not be afraid my grandson. You will learn about Turtle and Coyote, and places you have seen. Tonight you will learn where the people came from in the beginning. You will learn why people suffer and why people die. All these things will be told you."

The Rainy Season

1. The Maidu Creation Story

"In the long ago the first land was at Durham. Here grew an oak tree which bore all kinds of acorns—acorns of the valley oak, live oak, and others. This tree was cut by whites a few years ago when clearing for the railroad. After this, many of our people died."

Maidu informant
Chico, 1919, as cited
by Merriam 1966:315

Inside the dance house at *Kadema* the fire crackled and smoked from the moisture in the wood on the night when the moon was fixed by Coyote. The *Yĕ'poni* elders of the *Ku'ksū* Secret Society sat by the fire with their youth inside the dance house at *Kadema*. They always sat facing the sacred spirit pole during the long winter nights, telling the young people the creation and other stories, but only at night so as not to bring bad luck.

In this manner, Tokiwa sat with five other boys in front of the fire hearth to learn from the headman, Tawec. His young friends were known to their people as Ah-wahn (Turtle), Ahk (Crow), He-lo' (Ground Squirrel), Juh-huhp (Lucky) and Pippa (Sweet Acorn Soup). They learned about animals and landmarks which they would encounter in nature, and received answers to questions, such as: Where did the people come from in the beginning? Why do the people suffer? Why do the people die? The wisdom and spiritual knowledge they gained helped to shape their character and personality.

Each masterful storyteller stood in turn to speak. Soon it was time for Tawec. Tokiwa and his friends listened eagerly, for they knew that Tawec was especially skilled in his art. His voice would rise and then fall, full of laughter and vitality, adopting the tone and manner of the characters in his stories. For a moment, Tawec stood in silence, for speech-making never began all at once, nor in a hurried manner. Only one voice was heard at a time. Tawec now spoke:

"My friends, I am going to tell you the story of creation exactly as told to me by my grandfather long ago. It is the story of all life which is holy, for you are the children of one

"Storyteller" by Maidu artist Dalbert S. Castro.

Spirit, the Good Spirit, who we also call Earth-Maker. If you listen to my story, you will learn in the way our elders learned, for it was the spirits who told our medicine people, our *yo-mi.*"

And then Tawec proceeded to tell the following story:

"In The Beginning," by Nisenan artist Harry Fonseca.

In the beginning all was dark, for there was no sun, no moon, no stars. Above there was sky and infinite air. Below lay a vast ocean of infinite water. There existed also the unseen line of the two opposing forces of Good and Evil. Where this unseen line was drawn, there was the ocean and the sky.

(Tawec paused momentarily.)

From the north, a raft came floating on the water eternal and forever bound. The raft revolved slowly, turning first this way and then that, forever pushed and pulled by unsettled currents of air, forced to play a whirling game of timelessness. Thus the raft forever traveled, each movement and every direction at the whim of the invisible forces of pre-creation.

Riding upon the raft were two spirits, Turtle and *Peheipe*, the clown and Father-of-the-Secret-Society. There was nothing else. Suddenly they heard distant sounds of splitting. They gazed around themselves and up into the skyward gloom. There, far above in their own grey sky, a hole appeared. Light came forth streaming out in many strange hues.

(The boys now became enthralled by Tawec's imagery. They leaned forward to hear his every word.)

Then, down through the ashen void a rope of feathers, called *Po-kelma*, was lowered to their raft. The rope end hovered just beside them.

The feather rope faded from view where the sight of eye could not clearly reach, where the sky was all aglow from the rupture still unknown, from which Earth-Maker, the flaming god, did descend.

(Tawec used his hands deftly to describe the scene.)

Hand over hand Earth-Maker traveled down the feathered rope until his shining body stepped down upon the raft. His face was covered and could not be seen, but his body and robes shone like the sun. Tying the rope to the bow of the raft, he straightened and pointed skyward, saying:

(Tawec's voice now deepened.)

"I come from above. I come from the upper world of timelessness."

Still wrapped within his flaming robes, Earth-Maker, the Creator, then settled to the center of the craft, his head thrust forward in concentrated thought. Thus he sat silent and unmoving, while the raft stopped upon the surging currents, swung and strained against its feathered mooring from the sky.

Years of silent thought passed by, but now the sense of time brought impatience, and impatience finally made Turtle speak:

(The storyteller's pitch changed for Turtle.)

"I cannot fly... no, and though I sometimes swim in the unseen water, I must ever rise for air. So I exist upon this raft; swimming in one and breathing the other. Is this then all there will ever be for me?"

Then *Peheipe*, feeling ever more impatient, shouted loudly:

(Tawec's voice raised in pitch to become Peheipe.)

"Is there no place where those who neither fly nor swim can be, besides this pitching raft that's never still? ... ever squeezed between the two unseen forces of Good and Evil?"

And Earth-Maker replied: "I am of the air, and to make the world of good dry earth, I need a ball of earth found only below these raging currents, far beneath this ocean scum."

On hearing this Turtle spoke again: "If you will tie a rope about my left arm, I'll dive to the bottom and get some."

Earth-Maker did as Turtle asked, and then, reaching around, took the end of a rope from somewhere and tied it to Turtle. Turtle then said:

"If the rope is not long enough, I'll jerk it once, and you must haul me up; if it is long enough, I'll give two jerks, and then you must pull me up quickly, as I shall be holding your ball of earth and this body will be weak and in pain for lack of air."

(Tawec and the boys glanced at one another in anticipation.)

With the sound of an invisible splash, Turtle disappeared into the greyness of the ocean. *Peheipe* began shouting loudly and Earth-Maker, seated straight and still, nodded wisely to himself.

Turtle, with his stomach full of air, hurled himself through the violent water. He fought downward through the upward surges, plunging past the whirling pools, through streams of heat and countless layers of thin ice, and fearful thoughts that live there in the deep.

At the end of the fourth year of his descent, Turtle found the water was taking on a greenish hue. It grew quiet, sluggish, thick, and still, until it became a jellied primal slime he struggled through.

First one arm and then the other, pulled him slithering still farther downward until at last he reached and touched the surface of that ever-drowned and ancient world. *(For effect, Tawec crouched down on his haunches and gently patted the floor before his silent audience, imitating Turtle.)*

Painfully Turtle searched across those stony plains. He scraped here and there with horny fingernails, and slowly he gathered in his arms a large soft ball of spongy earth. Finally, with a tortured groan, Turtle pulled twice upon the rope.

The rope jerked taut snatching Turtle upward, shooting him through the green and ashen waters. *(Tawec jumped in the air.)* The last of Turtle's breath, escaping with his groan, became a curving trail of silver bubbles rising with him from the receding gloom.

Finally, with the sound of spray and hungry gasps, Turtle burst to the surface, clothed in streaming tresses of greenish slime. He heaved himself upon the raft and fell.

In despair he held out his empty hands . . . Sadly, in the two years of that upward journey, the jealous waters had stripped the earthen ball from his arms!

Then Earth-Maker drew an obsidian knife from deep within the folds of his great robe, and carefully scraped the earth out from under Turtle's horny nails. As each nail was scraped clean, Earth-Maker gathered each tiny pile of earth that fell into the center of his palm, and with a finger of his other hand he rolled the earth round and round into a tiny earthen ball as large as a small pebble.

Placing that soft round pebble on the stern of the raft, the Creator stood and spoke at last:

(Tawec rose off his heels, leaned forward and continued.) "An earthen ball of any size will do."

Then Earth-Maker once more settled to the center of the raft and closed his eyes in power-filled thought. Twice within that time his eyes came open and his gaze bore hard upon the earthen pebble. By the third such gaze the earth had grown to a size much larger than that which Turtle had gathered on the ocean floor.

When the Creator gazed upon the earthen pebble the fourth time, it had grown as large as the world is now, causing the raft to come aground at *Ta'doikö*, and all around were mountains as far as he could see.

(Tawec, the storyteller, stood back and pointed north with his finger.)

When the raft had come to land, Turtle said: "I can't stay in the dark all the time, can't you make a light, so that I can see?"

Earth-Maker replied: "Let us get out of the raft, and then we will see what we can do."

So all three got out. Earth-Maker lifted his hand up towards the faint tiers of mountain range and spoke: "Look that way, to the east! I am going to tell my sister to come up. She will give you warmth and light."

There, from the east in an ever widening glow, the first day came. A ball of fire lifted from the mountain peaks and swung slowly into the sky.

Turtle asked, "Which way is the sun going to travel?"

Earth-Maker answered while making a wide sweep with his arm from east to west across the sky. "I'll tell her to go this way, and to go down there."

After the sun went down, *Peheipe*, Father-of-the-Secret Society, began to cry and shout loudly, for it grew very dark.

Earth-Maker said, "Look then to the east. I'll tell my brother, the moon, to come up."

From the east a sharp-edged sphere of orange and

yellow rose to cross the pure black dome of the sky, spreading soft and cooling light upon the earth. Then, with a wide sweep of his arm, and calling each by name, Earth-Maker caused every star to shine.

At last Turtle looked about and said, "All that has been done is good. Is this then all that you will do for us, or is there more that we shall see and know?"

Then Earth-Maker, the Creator of everything, reaching again into the folds of his ever flaming robe, spoke once more, "The time is near to begin that for which the world was made—the time is near for life to grow."

Earth-Maker extended an upturned palm and displayed a shiny greenish oblong ball no bigger than his thumb saying "Here is *Ooti*, the acorn, taken from the Upper Meadow. I have brought her with me from heaven. Into the earth I will place this seed of good."

Kneeling on the ground at *Ta'doikö*, Earth-Maker scooped a shallow hole from the earth. He placed the polished seed there and returned the earth over it. He then caused the world's first rain and heavy clouds of steam to rise that curled from the sea and spread over the earth. With the earth now moist and sweet, *Ooti* the acorn sprouted and grew into a very large tree with rough and gullied bark on its outer trunk and sturdy limbs bearing flat green leaves and twelve different kinds of acorns.

Then they sat for two days and rested beneath the shade of the acorn tree. Refreshed, Earth-Maker, Turtle and *Peheipe* set out to see and marvel at the world that Earth-Maker had made. They started their travels at sunrise, but so quickly did Earth-Maker guide them that all they could see was a ball of fire flashing about under the ground and in the water.

In their absence, Coyote and his friend, "Dog" Rattlesnake, rose up out of the ground. Coyote came squirming up through the earth and sat panting. *(Tawec now walked, looking ridiculous. The boys, watched and giggled. Tawec continued but with warning now in his voice.)*

Coyote could see Earth-Maker's face. At sunset as the dusk settled over the land, the three returned to the acorn tree at *Ta'doikö*, and Earth-Maker, seeing Coyote seated by the tree with his face full of smirks and grins, turned to Turtle and *Peheipe* and said, "Coyote is of the air as I am, yet his body bears an earth-like coat. It is he that many will call Evil."

All five of them then built lodges for themselves and lived there at *Ta'doikö*, but no one could go inside Earth-maker's house.

Soon afterwards, Earth-Maker wandered here and there scattering seeds in the four directions to clothe the world in grasses, brush and trees. He then passed his hand through the air and filled the sky with birds. He created all the animals too. Sometimes Turtle would say, "That does not look well. Can't you make it some other way?"

In this way the earth was filled with life.

Some time after this, Earth-Maker and Coyote were at *Esto-Yamani*, the "middle hills." They stood upon the highest and most sacred peak of *Esto-Yamani* where the valley wind, rising hot and fast, moaned over the blackened stones. As this wind whipped the flaming hair about his upturned head, Earth-Maker spoke to forces and to spirits that he alone could see. "Now I will finish that for which the world was made. Now I shall give life to mankind, that he may use all that has been created. I am going to make the people."

In the middle of the afternoon he began, after his return to *Ta'doikö*. Taking dark red earth, he mixed it with water, and made two figures, one a man and one a woman. He laid the man on his right side and the woman on his left, inside his house. Then he lay down himself, flat on his back, with his arms stretched outwards. He lay thus and sweated all the afternoon and night. Early in the morning he felt the woman begin to tickle him in the side. He kept very still and did not laugh.

By and by he got up, thrust a piece of pitchwood into the ground and fire burst out. The two people were very white. No one today is as white as they were. Their eyes were pink, their hair was black, and their teeth shone brightly. They were very handsome.

Earth-Maker did not finish the hands of the people, for he did not know how it would be best to do it. Little Lizard came out from the ground and finding Coyote, held his hands out and said, "Ssssssst! Man should have five fingers like mine."

Coyote ran after Little Lizard. Back in the hole he went. Coyote swore and tamped dirt all around the hole, but he knew he could not kill Little Lizard. So he went down the hill again.

Out from the ground again came Little Lizard. "Ssssssst! Man must have five fingers like I have."

Coyote was so mad, he just kept going. But Little Lizard won his point, and that's why humans have hands like his.

This first man was called *Ku'ksū*, and the woman, Morning Star Woman.

Seeing the two people Coyote asked Earth-Maker how he had made them. When he was told, Coyote thought, That is not difficult. I'll do it myself.

Coyote mixed the earth into red mud and took it inside his house. He shaped a man and woman figures. Coyote laid them out on either side of him, and then lay down on his back between them. Keeping a fire going, he lay sweating with his arms stretched outwards all the afternoon and night. Early in the morning, the woman figure poked him in the ribs. As a result, Coyote wiggled and then laughed. He could not help laughing. As a result of Coyote's failure to keep still, the man and woman became glassy-eyed.

Earth-Maker walked into Coyote's lodge and saw the glassy-eyed figures. He said, "I told you not to laugh."

Coyote, who knew what Evil is, and always does it first, turned towards the Earth-Maker, looked into his eyes and declared he had not. Thus the first lie was told in the world.

Earth-Maker then went back to his house and went into a deep study. The Creator made up his mind then about Coyote, but remained in seclusion, occasionally visiting and confiding only in *Ku'ksū* at night. Earth-Maker wanted to have everything comfortable and easy for the people, so that none of them should have to work. All fruits were easy to obtain. No one was ever to get sick and die. One night the Earth-Maker came to *Ku'ksū* and said to him, "The line between the two opposing forces is drawn. To-morrow morning you must go to the little lake near here, and take all the people with you. *Ku'ksū*, I'll make you a very old man before you get to the lake. It will be to teach Coyote. When you emerge from the water your lips will have my voice. You will have no life apart from me. You will pass on that which I want known."

Ku'ksū did as he was told. In the morning he collected all the people and went to the lake. On the way there, *Ku'ksū* lost his youthful gait. Gradually his strong hands and handsome face became gnarled with wrinkles like the trunk of the acorn tree. *(Tawec, the storyteller, distorted his face with both hands.)* *Ku'ksū's* jet black hair turned willowly and white. He had turned into a very old man. Staggering, *Ku'ksū* fell into the lake with a big splash. He sank out of sight. There was quiet.

Pretty soon the people could feel the ground shake. They saw the lake now alive with waves that came crashing on the shore. And there was a great roaring from under the water that sounded like thunder. By and by, *Ku'ksū* came up out of the water, but most marvelous of all, just like a young man again.

Then Earth-Maker came and spoke to the people, and said, "If you do as I tell you, everything will be well. When any of you grow old, so old that you cannot walk, come to this lake or get someone to bring you here." When he had said this, he went away. He left in the night, climbing the feathered rope to the Upper World.

All this time food had been easily obtained, as Earth-Maker had wished. The women set out baskets at night, and in the morning they found them full of food, all ready to eat, and lukewarm. The acorns were sweet and good, so it was easy to make bread and soup.

One day Coyote came along with his friends Skunk and "Dog" Rattlesnake. Coyote asked the people how they lived, and they told him that all they had to do was to eat and sleep. Coyote, Skunk, and "Dog" Rattlesnake sat down together. Coyote said, "The women do not have enough to do, so they talk too much, and get into trouble. We must do something about it."

They thought a long time. Then "Dog" Rattlesnake said, "Skunk must spray the trees and make the acorns bitter with skunk scent."

Coyote said, "That is good! Skunk, you do it."

Skunk did just that. *(Tawec then made like a skunk and the boys all laughed at what he was imitating.)*

No longer was it easy to prepare the acorn soup. Women had much work to do to wash this skunk scent away from the acorn flour. The bitter water washed from the ground-up acorn was the color of Coyote.

Skunk sprayed the buckeye trees too, so they also would have a skunk scent. From that time on the fruits of the oak and buckeye were inedible without washing.

Coyote went before the people and spoke, "This is still no way to be. I can show you something better."

He told them that he and Earth-Maker had had a discussion before the people had been made, how Earth-

Maker had wanted everything easy, and that there should be no work, sickness or death, but how Coyote had thought it would be better to have people work, get sick, and die. He then told the people what he had done to the acorn and buckeye and announced, "When the people die, let them die forever. Then there will be a burning."

The people couldn't understand, what Coyote meant by this. But Coyote said, "I'll show you. It is better to have a burning, for then the widows can be free."

He then fixed the moon and took all the baskets and things that the people had and hung them on poles and made everything ready. When all was prepared, Coyote said, "At this time you must always have games, for we can all have a good time at the cry."

Then Coyote laid out games to be played and the course for a foot-race. Coyote told them, "You must start the games with a foot-race, so get ready to run." *(Tawec then made ready like he was about to run.)*

Everyone got set at the course except *Ku'ksū*. He sat in his hut alone, and was sad, for he *knew* what was going to come into the world. Earth-Maker had confided in *Ku'ksū* that Coyote should be the first mourner.

Just at this moment "Dog" Rattlesnake came to *Ku'ksū* and said, "What shall we do now? Everything is spoiled!" *Ku'ksū* did not answer, so "Dog" Rattlesnake smirked, "Well, I'll do what I think is best."

Then he went out along the course which the racers were to go over. He hid himself, leaving his head just sticking out of a hole.

By this time all the racers had started. Among them was Coyote's son. He was Coyote's only child, and he was very quick. He soon began to outstrip all the runners, and took the lead. As he passed the spot where "Dog" Rattlesnake had hidden himself, Rattlesnake raised his head and bit this first runner in the ankle. In a minute the boy was dead.

Coyote was dancing about the homestake. *(Tawec imitated this.)* He was very happy, shouting at his son and praising him. When Rattlesnake bit the boy causing him to fall, everyone laughed at Coyote saying, "Your son has fallen down, and is so ashamed that he does not dare to get up."

Coyote said, "No, that is not it. He is dead."

The people, however, did not understand. Picking the boy up, they brought him to Coyote. Then Coyote began to cry to show the people, and everyone did the same. These were the first tears for the first death.

Coyote took his son's body and carried it to the lake of which Earth-Maker had told them, and threw the body in, causing a splash. But there was no noise, and nothing happened. The boy drifted about for four days on the surface, like a dog. Something is wrong, Coyote thought.

On the fifth day Coyote took four sacks of beads and brought them to *Ku'ksū*. He begged him to restore his son to life, for he had come back to life himself and all had seen this.

Ku'ksū did not answer. For five days Coyote begged and still *Ku'ksū* did not answer. On the last day, with Coyote still begging, *Ku'skū* then came out of his house. He brought all his beads and bearskins, and called to all the people and to Coyote to come and watch him. He laid the body on a bearskin, dressed it, and wrapped it up carefully. Then he dug a grave, put the body into it, and covered it up. Then he told all, "From now on, this is what you must do. This is the way you must do until the world shall be made over."

But Coyote protested how this could not happen to him; that it was only for the people to suffer and die.

About a year after this, in the spring, all was changed. Up to this time everybody spoke the same language. The people were having a "second burning" celebration.

"Why Moon?" by Maidu artist Dalbert S. Castro.

Everything was ready for the next day, when in the night everybody suddenly began to speak a different language. Only each man and his wife spoke the same tongue. Earth-Maker had come in the night to *Ku'ksū*, and had told him about it all, and given him more instructions for the next day.

So, when morning came, *Ku'ksū* called all the people together, for he was able to speak all the languages. He told them each the names of the different animals, and so forth in their languages, taught them how to cook and to hunt, gave them all their laws, and set the time for all their dances and festivals. Then he called each tribe by name, and set them off in different directions, telling them where they were to live. He sent the warriors to the north, the singers to the west, the flute-players to the east, and the dancers to the south. So all the people went away, leaving in the night, going first to *Esto-Yamani*, the "middle hills." *Ku'ksū* stayed a little while longer, and then he also left.

At *Esto-Yamani*, the Earth-Maker worked. There he made a rope of white feathers reaching from the top of the mountain up to the Milky Way in the sky. This was a road, and it was called the Road of the Dead. After finishing the road, the Creator prepared Coyote's son to travel the road. The Creator then took the spirit out of Coyote's son, leaving his body.

All this time, Coyote had been trying to find out where *Ku'ksū* had gone, and where his own son had gone. At last he found his tracks, and followed them to the *Ka'kinim Kumi*, spirit house. It was evening when Coyote reached the mountain sweathouse and the door was on the west. It was half open. He saw his son there, sitting on the north side. *Ku'ksū* was sitting on the ground by the center post of the sweathouse eating *Ka'kinim pe* (spirit food).

Coyote wanted to go in, but *Ku'ksū* said, "No. Wait there. You cannot come into this sweathouse unless you die. You have just what you wanted. It is your own fault. You yourself wished things to be this way. Now you have what you wished.

"Every man will now have all kinds of troubles and accidents, will have to work to get his food, and will die and be buried.

"This must go on 'till the time is out, and Earth-Maker comes again, and everything will be made over.

"And now you go back to your house and tell all that you have seen. Tell them that you have seen your son, that he is not dead. Tell them that none of your people can ever come into this spirit house until they die."

Coyote said he would go, but that he was hungry and wanted some of the food. *Ku'ksū* replied, "You cannot eat that. Only ghosts may eat that food."

So Coyote started for home and while he was gone *Ku'ksū*, according to the Creator's instructions, took the spirit of Coyote's son on the road to the sky, or heaven.

When Coyote was within sight of his home he began shouting, "I have seen my son and *Ku'ksū*, and he told me to kill myself. They are in a good place with plenty to eat."

After all this, Earth-Maker thought it best that he should have someone to guard the mountain spirit house. So *Peheipe*, also known as the clown, was placed on the very top of the spirit house in order that the dead would be guided by the voice of this clown. Earth-Maker gave the clown the power to know when anyone had died, and even to know their names. In calling them he could say, "Come this way! Don't get lost! Don't go that way! Be careful how you step."

The Creator also left a man at the door of the mountain house so that when the dead came he could remove the clothing in which they were buried and prepare them for the feather road which only the dead may travel.

After Coyote had told all, he was anxious to die, for he wished to go to the beautiful place he had seen. He planned to climb a tree and kill himself by falling. But after climbing the tree, he saw so many people around that he was ashamed, and decided that he would live. But that same night he again wanted to die, so he climbed up into the same tree and fell off, breaking his neck. Next morning he was found dead, and his people took him and buried him.

So Coyote went to the place he was so anxious to see. But there was no one there, no food, nothing at all. It was because he had come into the spirit house in such a sneaky way—by killing himself.

Some say Coyote walked away temporarily to the west; that he never left the Earth and rules the entire world to this day. *Ku'ksū* and Coyote's son, however, have gone on the feather road up into the sky.

There are conflicting stories about where the Creator has gone. Some say he has gone to the north, where he will live forever. Others have a different story; that he has gone—like *Ku'ksū* and the Coyote's son—through the hole to his home far above in the sky, but will someday return when the time is out and everything will be made over.

○ ○ ○

Tawec, the headman and storyteller, then looked at the boys, "That is all," he said.

2. The Ku'ksū Secret Society

"Who's tending this sun, moon?
Who moves them around?
There must be somebody to look
after this world."

Nisenan informant
Beals 1933:380

In the *Yamanködö* encampment just up river from *Kadema*, the main village, it was vacation time, a period when Tokiwa and the other Secret Society initiates could be outside rather than shut inside the ceremonial sweat lodge. That first morning of vacation, when Tokiwa raised his head from under his rabbit-skin blanket, his thoughts normally would run at once to the scent of the acorn cooking and deer meat broiling in the quiet morning.

But not today.

An urge more powerful than appetite surged through his body. Tokiwa was thinking again of pretty Nesuya. She was the daughter of Big Meadows, the hunting captain of the community. He lay there picturing her smooth, round body. He saw her alluring smile and big brown eyes.

Most beguiling about Nesuya were the three, thin tattoo marks, which ran vertically on her chin, blue from the juice of a flower. For Tokiwa, who had grown up with

Nesuya, the three marks created an entirely new set of symbols. Always before her chin had been unmarked, her body undeveloped. Now she was beautified, and became to him a seductive woman.

Publicly, of course, it was known that she had passed through her first menses, and, by tradition, had isolated herself in a lodge for sixteen days. During those days she had never been allowed outside alone. On the sixteenth day she had been marked with the blue "lll" and bathed.

More memories presented themselves. Back in that flower month, Tokiwa remembered how they had played a wonderful game of foot ball. The women had played against the men, who put up valuables, such as baskets, clothes, and bags of clamshells to bet with each other. They had run in a relay fashion in which each team tried to kick and carry its own stuffed buckskin ball to a goal half a mile away and then back again to the starting point.

Then Tokiwa recalled the harsh words he had had with Ya-hai-lum who had insulted him that day. Ya-hai-lum was the star player for *Pusuni*, the large village complex down at the mouth of the river where the *No'to-mom* emptied into Big River. Tokiwa was itching to win the game that day.

Tokiwa told Ya-hai-lum, "I bet one string of shell beads that we will win." Ya-hai-lum, who was lanky and sinewy, fifteen years older than Tokiwa and still a very good athlete, accepted the bet. He was a runner and "brave man" fighter for the *Pusuni* brother-chiefs and was very smart. But Ya-hai-lum was also shifty and cocky and, worse yet, a womanizer. Tokiwa noticed how, throughout the matches, his eyes fell constantly upon Nesuya.

"That new woman, Nesuya, is a beauty," he grinned. "Do you want to place another bet that her parents will like me?" Ya-hai-lum asked Tokiwa.

Angered, Tokiwa remained silent. He didn't want to encourage Ya-hai-lum in any way. But Ya-hai-lum could see the inner struggle on Tokiwa's face. He began laughing.

"You care for Nesuya!" he snickered. "Why you don't even hunt well, boy."

Tokiwa raised his eyebrows and glared back at Ya-hai-lum, "He who is the constant talker is considered rude and unthinking."

Soon the foot ball game began.

The men kicked the ball with the foot, while the women caught it with their hands and ran with it. When Nesuya was tackled, Ya-hai-lum tickled Nesuya's belly. She, in turn, threw the ball to another woman. Tokiwa wished he dared do the same but he was too shy.

They played this way together so that a man could hug the woman he loved. The women on their part took every opportunity to hug the men they loved. It was this experience that Tokiwa woke up remembering. He also remembered losing his bet that day.

Tokiwa, alone inside his family's lodge, wrapped his rabbit-skin blanket, trimmed with grey squirrel tails, into a roll. With eyes closed, he pretended the blanket was Nesuya, her cuddly body caught up in his arms. In fond hopes, he repeated again and again how he would throw pretty Nesuya to the ground and roll her around with his face buried in her warm accepting breasts.

He thought how someday he might have Nesuya as a wife of his own to do his bidding—something he had never considered because he was young. Nevertheless Tokiwa knew the importance of a wife of one's own: to be served a good breakfast and a good supper whenever he was home; to have someone making baskets and grinding acorns; to collect bulbs, tender greens, and roots while he was away hunting; to share the warmth of the fur blankets during the nights. He knew he wanted to be responsible and deserving, for only a good man could get a good woman and neither could be lazy.

Tokiwa arose that morning eating only acorn soup which his mother had prepared for him. He gathered more firewood and then joined up with Pippa and Ah-wahn', two other initiate boys, and together they headed for the lake across the river to collect the *ó-ldo*, or marsh reeds, for arrow shafts.

Tokiwa, in his seventeenth summer, was a sturdily built young man. He stood five feet seven inches and had a full mouth and small dark eyes. His face was broad and his cheekbones were prominent. Tokiwa's long straight, black hair was held back by a narrow band of mink fur. Other than his breechcloth of deerskin, he was naked and barefoot. His people needed no footwear.

Tokiwa, Pippa and Ah-wahn', along with Ahk, He-lo', and Juh-huhp, were boys-becoming men. They had been undergoing initiation ceremonies for the last few months. They were all new initiates of the *Ku'ksū* Secret Society and hoped soon to become *Yĕ'poni* or full members. The purpose of the Secret Society was to initiate boys into the proper ways of manhood and to keep the dance house and sacred rites as Earth-Maker had commanded. Today, their manhood training required them to make a bow and arrows.

At the lake, Ahk, He-lo', and Juh-huhp had already arrived and were busy collecting reeds. Everyone had gathered enough materials by mid-morning. They met So-se-yah-mah, Tokiwa's grandfather, at a quiet place upriver. So-se-yah-mah was one of their teachers. His beautiful sinew-backed bow and quiver filled with arrows rested against the trunk of the great gnarled oak under which they worked.

Pride shone in the wrinkled, brown face of So-se-yah-mah, the tribal dance leader who lived at *Yamanködö* with Tokiwa and his mother, Woyectena. The boys worked separately in a wide circle, strictly supervised by the old man. They continued to fletch arrows, splitting three red-tailed hawk feathers for each arrow. So-se-yah-mah had previously shown the boys how to further bind the feathers at the butt end of the arrow by lashing with more sinew. This way the feathers would never fall off.

So-se-yah-mah walked over to Tokiwa. He approved of what he saw in his grandson, who had just finished winging another arrow. "Grandson, you do well with your feathers. Not everyone can use feathers right. There are different kinds of feathers and different kinds of birds and different kinds of dreams. Some are powerful and some are not."

"What kinds of dreams are powerful, Grandfather?" Tokiwa asked. "How can I tell?"

"Ho! Like powerful feathers, there are those dreams that are more important than the others. They are given to you a little differently. The dreams shared by ghost spirits are the ones which are most powerful, my grandson. These dream spirits provide doorways to many things if you listen. But you must only listen, for in that moment when a human being speaks to a ghost he dies."

Whenever in a training session with an elder, all the boys came to anticipate that they would receive sacred teachings, for the boys were now initiates and that is what *Yĕ'poni* grandfathers were for. Grandparents spent more time with the children than the parents, who were often away from home, either hunting, fishing or gathering roots, nuts, and berries. So-se-yah-mah was thus responsible to direct Tokiwa and the other boys along the path towards becoming a *Yĕ'poni*.

So-se-yah-mah stood facing all six initiates. "Listen, listen, my children," he said. "This place, *Yamanködö*, is a place of power. Look at the water which moves here."

Together they walked out onto the river bank where they could see the swirling white-water swells. Only here, along the river could such rapids be found. Downstream, and for a long way upstream, the river was smooth and placid.

"The many water riffles are inhabited by a spirit being named *Unai* who comes from the Lower World and drowns people by holding them down," So-se-yah-mah explained.

"In the beginning, the Lower World, along with the Upper and Middle Worlds, were the three realms into which Earth-Maker had cast out power. The Lower World is the home of beings who are malevolent and live close to water, springs, underground rivers and caves. The Upper World is occupied by Earth-Maker, Sun, Moon, and certain star constellations, as well as the dead people in the Heavenly Valley above. The Middle World consists of all the living people on the earth and some non-mortal beings, such as *ku'ksū* [not capitalized here to distinguish from *Ku'ksū* used previously], the wood spirit who has only one leg and one eye. This *ku'ksū* lurks in the woods and causes travelers who encounter him to bleed from the nose and mouth.

"You must remember these things because you are boys-becoming-men now."

"What does *Unai* look like, Grandfather?" Pippa asked.

"*Unai* is part human and part fish. The sound of his voice is the cry of a baby. Sometimes I have seen *Unai* in the afternoons reclining on the bank. When I run quickly to that place I can see traces where he had left the water. I find the water boiling where *Unai* has jumped in and disappeared."

Never before had Tokiwa so wanted to see a super-natural being. But in learning about *Unai*, he and the other initiates gained greater respect for the water. In learning about *ku'ksū*, the boys paid greater attention to the surrounding woodlands.

They walked together for some time in silence. Together they stared out into the deeper, green-blue water—eternal, forever moving, forever powerful.

A sudden wind then blew across the river stirring the great oak. The boys noticed So-se-yah-mah's concern, for the wind was a warning. He stood looking up to the tree, listening. "Better stay away from the water," So-se-yah-mah warned. "It's best to return to bow and arrow making."

"Bow-making is a craft of which only a few are knowledgeable," the Grandfather said. "Bows are made of yew wood, obtained in the higher country."

As he spoke, So-se-yah-mah demonstrated how the wood was carefully split and dried, and then scraped and smoothed, using jointed grass. When this was completed, So-se-yah-mah showed the boys how to back the bow with deer sinew laid lengthwise obtained from the back strap of a deer.

"Initiates, the sinew is applied to give the bow added spring. It is applied by first smearing the bow with salmon's nose cooked in the ashes. The salmon's juices serve as a glue. If you don't have salmon, the air bladder of sturgeon can be used."

After their midday meal, So-se-yah-mah pulled back the deer sinew bow string. The bow was still a little too stiff, so he instructed Ahk to scrape the bow until it was limber.

Using a feather tip, they applied a greenish-blue pigment to the bow to make a snake design. The color was traded from their Achumawi neighbors to the north. "This will give the bow more power," So-se-yah-mah explained. "Your bow will have the striking power of the rattlesnake."

Nisenan bows were highly prized by neighboring groups. The best trade could be made with the Mona to the east. In barter, the Mona provided their scoop-shaped, seedbeater baskets, which looked very much like the Nisenan's twined wicker-work basket. They were used in the popular game called *ama-ty* played by women.

Headman Tawec was readying a trade expedition to the

Mona country. This winter So-se-yah-mah had made five bows to be traded on this trip, although he was too old to go. After the trading, they would stay with the Mountain Maidu to participate in the Bear Dance. This expedition would have to travel cautiously. On the way, they might run into some bitter *Chucumnes* across the river to the south. Trading was forbidden with them now that fighting had worsened. *Chucumnes* had killed his father when Tokiwa was a newborn, and now, by custom, he carried his late father's name.

"Those *Chucumnes* are bad," Woyectena, the boy's mother would lament. "It is the *Chucumnes* who are the aggressors. They cross the river to attack and kill hunting parties of our people."

Woyectena added, "And the *Moan-au-zi* are no better. They come over the mountains armed with wooden knives, with which they kill our people. They scalp them. I wish that every snake which ever lived would bite them all."

The next day, Tokiwa and his five fellow initiates met with So-se-yah-mah to make more arrows. "The arrow length must be as long as the bow. This makes for greater distance when shooting," Grandfather explained.

The boys scraped the *o'-ldo* reeds they had left in bundles to dry. Once dry, they would straighten these reed shafts by heating each arrow over a fire and then passing each through a hole they had bored through the fork of a deer's antler. By a treatment of wrenching, twisting, and holding each arrow, they made the shafts straight.

"We will now go see Nunco, the village arrowhead maker. We will promise him some of our meat in exchange for his arrowheads."

Old Nunco was found working near the front of his lodge. He looked up momentarily when the boys and Grandfather arrived. "The most desired stone for flaking arrowheads is *wa-se*, the black, volcanic rock," So-se-yah-mah said.

Everyone watched as old Nunco purposefully shattered some of the obsidian cores against harder stones until an appropriate hand-size piece was knocked off. He carefully set this razor sharp piece atop a piece of deer neck leather. Holding the stone as still as possible, he meticulously notched away against the obsidian piece by carefully applying pressure with a sharpened deer antler point. These arrowheads old Nunco presented to the initiates.

They now fastened the arrowheads to shafts with thin strips of moistened deer sinew which each boy bound round and round the butt end of the arrow shaft and the neck of the arrowhead. When dry, they applied melted pine gum mixed with charcoal as an added reinforcement.

Lastly, each hunter marked his own arrow for purposes of identification. Tokiwa chose a white painted long groove in honor of the great white goose called "God's bird."

Tokiwa thought about the exacting strictness required by the people for every aspect of life, such as basketry and feather work. If each feather was not perfectly scraped and set in the prescribed direction on the arrows, or if the arrowheads were not fashioned in the proper manner, the elders would say, "The objects must be buried."

Properly crafted bows and arrows made by the initiates were proof that they had finished part of their training into the Secret Society. Fortunately no one's work was buried. But this was only one important part of training, as Tokiwa and the other new initiates knew full well.

Not all men could go through initiation; only those whose names the head doctor had received from the voices of spirits. Older Ya-hai-lum, for instance, had never been named. He had made quite a big stir in the *Kadema* dance house that spring. Tokiwa and the five other boys had just been announced. Ya-hai-lum had stood up from where he was sitting.

"Why is it that the spirits have not seen it proper for

me to train to become the *Yĕ'poni*? I run fast and am never wicked," Ya-hai-lum protested.

Tawec stood by Big Meadows and Old-Grouse Woman, the head doctor. "Perhaps it is because you have bad manners when around the women and that you are accused of stealing feathers," Tawec responded.

"Who says I steal sacred feathers?" Ya-hai-lum protested with knitted eyebrows.

Big Meadows, the *Kadema* hunting captain, then stepped forward. He stood six feet five inches tall and had a massive body. He smiled confidently, and responded seriously. "It is I who saw you do this, Ya-hai-lum. Have you truly forgotten?"

"Big Meadows, that was over twelve months ago. Have I not made good this wrong that bothers you?"

The elders looked at one another. With silent understanding they remained firm in their decision.

Tokiwa was pleased with this turn of events. Families regarded all *Yĕ'poni* highly, as it was believed they brought good luck to the family. With Ya-hai-lum kept out Tokiwa would have a distinct advantage in winning over Nesuya's father, Big Meadows, and Wypooke, her mother, when he graduated.

Ya-hai-lum had more to say to Big Meadows. "Your brother, Matos. I know him well in *Pusuni.* I know his heart. He says you have been conspiring against me. He is right. It is not the spirits who have denied my name, but rather all of you." Glaring angrily at Big Meadows and the elders, Ya-hai-lum turned on his heels and left the group.

At first, Tokiwa and his five friends had mixed thoughts about joining the Secret Society, for they had heard fearful stories of the doings inside the dance house during training sessions. Initiates who hoped to become *Yĕ'poni* would be confined inside the sweat-houses—boys for one full year and girls for six months. They would be allowed few short "vacation" periods.

At the same time, some of the older members were persuasive and used strenuous arguments to bring in youngsters with whom they were acquainted. One night a party of elders, carrying flaming pitch-pine torches, approached Tokiwa and three of the other boys, Pippa, Ah-wahn', and He-lo'.

"If you do not join, you will all be devoured by bears and mountain lions," stated one in the group.

"You will fall over precipices while hiking in the mountains or you will drown upon falling into the streams," warned another.

The leader of the group was So-me-lah, one of the *Kadema* dance house *Peheipes*. He had lots of influence and said, "Boys, if you don't begin your training on time, you will surely suffer death in one of these three ways. Worse yet, your spirits will go to the spirit-land by the left-hand path. This path leads to eternal darkness, while the right-hand path leads to light."

This convinced four of the boys to begin their initiation, while the other two soon followed.

As candidates, they were watched closely by the *Yē'poni* lodge officers who studied their ways, their natures, and conduct to determine if each was suitable. In addition to sacred rituals, they learned manners, hunting and fishing skills, how to make speeches, and the arts of medicine and foreseeing the future.

Some learned how to be *Peheipes*, clowns, or to be dance leaders like So-se-yah-mah. Often several clowns served one community as leaders. They served as sentries, directors of daily activites, and custodians of the fire and dance house. It was the *Peheipe's* task to "capture" young boys to become initiates. In everything, the *Peheipe's* duty was also to maintain the posture and antics of Coyote; to make puns and parodies to make people laugh so they could learn from life.

Tokiwa and all the initiates were obligated to participate in elaborate ceremonies involving fasts and instruction in the myths and lore of the tribe told by the older men. Finally, a great feast and dance would be held, at which time the neophytes would first perform their crafts and dances.

Graduating from the preliminary lodges was the first test. The young charges had to remain in the dance house by day and could only leave at night. They missed their families. When they went outside, they covered their faces with deer hide and then were taken out one at a time by the older Yĕ'poni. Their "home" was behind the foot drum. They brought in wood and water. They could eat no meat nor any grease. They could not take sweats or baths. They ate two meals a day of acorn soup and bread prepared by their mothers and sisters, and drank water.

After three weeks of living in this manner, the initiates participated in a sweat. The smoke hole of the sweat-house was covered up. It was to see how much they could endure. Some fainted but they were obligated to remain inside.

One day the door to the dance house was sealed, the fire reduced to coals by cold ashes being tossed across the flame. The Peheipe ornamented Tokiwa and the others with dancing regalia. He gave each boy a hairnet adorned with white goose-wing feathers which hung down over their faces and covered their eyes. The elders wrapped a girdle hung with hawk and owl feathers round their waists front and back. The Yĕ'poni leaders also presented each boy a wand which each one hung on the wall above his bed. The Peheipe daubed the faces of the youths with white clay overlaid with black stripes. They also placed black stripes on their wrists. Finally, they sprinkled acorn powder on the head of each boy, not to be washed off for four times four days, four being the number associated with all sacred matters.

During this confinement, *Peheipe* So-me-lah pierced the youths' ears and noses with cedar splinters. The nose incisions hurt the most. Ear and nose plugs were attached to the orifices, serving later to designate the men as full-fledged *Yĕ'poni*.

Another day the boys were "tested with arrows" to make brave men of them. A good level place was chosen and the boys were shot at from a short distance to teach them how to dodge arrows and keep their nerve under fire. Individually, they had to stand up to the volleys and dodge the arrows as well as they could.

The anxiety of each initiate was severe because the testing with arrows had to take place four different times, each trial being one month apart, and death was a very possible result of an error! Fortunately, none of Tokiwa's class of initiates so far had been killed. But everyone remembered well, in one training session the year before, one very young initiate was killed. When it happened, he was laid out on the ground and covered with valuables. Then he was burned, and his ashes were scraped together with his charred bones, then placed into a small basket and buried.

When Tokiwa's turn came, he was very nervous, but tried not to show anyone his fear. He went to the end of the open place, knowing full well that it would be So-se-yah-mah who would be shooting at him. Only Tokiwa's relatives could shoot their arrows, for the family might become angry if any non-family member should ever hit their mark. If Grandfather should unfortunately hit and kill him, there would be grief but no anger.

Tokiwa's biggest dread was that Grandfather was every bit as good an archer as he was a dance captain. A *Yĕ'poni* yelled "Shoot away." Intently, Tokiwa watched his Grandfather's every move. Tokiwa felt as though his heart was in his throat. His heart raced. So-se-yah-mah was silent and expressionless. First, Grandfather placed an arrow to his bowstring. Now he slowly raised up the bow and point of his arrow and aimed it while pulling back the bowstring. There! . . . There! the arrow was coming! It whizzed right for his knees. Tokiwa jumped this way, dodging the first arrow. This was repeated for what seemed a long time, again and again. Finally today's testing was over. Tokiwa had proven himself brave. The others congratulated him.

Girls were also given training. Only virgins between the ages twelve and seventeen could be selected. Nesuya had finished her training in her thirteenth year. Inside the dance house, she and the other girls were kept apart and closely watched by the *Peheipe*. They were permitted to go out twice a day under the watchful eyes of the oldest girl. They slept on one side, the boys on the other, with the *Peheipe* and *Yĕ'poni* in the center.

Nesuya and the other girls were drilled everyday in the dance. They had to dance before having a meal in the morning, tightening up the belts they wore. They learned which foods were permitted and which were forbidden. They learned how to care for themselves at the first menstruation. And how during these periods to never touch any object, food or otherwise, used by men; and to bath with wormwood always on finishing menstruation. The *Peheipe* instructed them in a discrete way.

"When you marry," the *Peheipe* told Nesuya and the other girls, "you must not eat in the presense of your husbands until the first child is born."

Their mothers repeated this instruction. Nesuya's mother cautioned her, "When you marry, respect your husband. You are not to eat with him. The first meal you eat face to face will be the occasion for a formal feast."

The old people taught Nesuya and the other girls, "You must take good care of your husband and not talk bad things. When he comes home from hunting, you must feed him right away. You must pound seeds and make flour so that he can drink that with his food when he comes home from hunting. You must talk of good things to him. When you sleep at night, don't play with him. If you play, he will get angry and beat you."

Whereas male initiates were "tested with arrows" four times, the girls were "tested with the dance" four times. Nesuya began her dance and finally when she finished an old man shouted to her, "Very good!" Nesuya paid the man with abalone shell and beads. Three times more she and the other girls danced. Each time the old man yelled "Very good!" and afterwards they paid him for his approval.

Tokiwa and the other five boys formed close bonds during the time of their initiation training. At the end of the twelfth month, they were released from the dance house. They looked pale and thin as their families met them. A large celebration feast was prepared and the boys were given meat again.

On this special day the boys dropped their child's name. They received their permanent names, which often were handed down from a dead *Yĕ'poni* relative. Tokiwa kept his father's name, while the other five received their permanent names. Pippa was renamed *Yo'to* or Woodpecker Head. An-wahn was named *Lo-lah'*, Big Wolf. Juh-huhp was no longer known as Lucky, but henceforth would be called *Ba-ba*, or Salt. Ahk's new name was *Tahmas*, Winter, and He-lo' dropped his nickname, Ground Squirrel, to become *Pahm-chahk*, Beaver.

Inside the dance house, headman Tawec came forward and stood by the spirit post and rubbed it, making a prayer to the four directions. He directed his prayers towards the south, the east, the north, and the west. Tawec spoke:

"I recite these instructions to all the new initiates, instructions given to the people by *Aikat*, the Creator.

"Never return to the brutish worship of your ancestors,

who prayed to the rocks, and rivers, and the hills; but rather pray to *Aikat,* the good and great spirit.

"Never wager men and women as your foolish ancestors did. In gambling, bet only such articles which are counted as property.

"Never forget or neglect the assembly-hall, the house of religion and the sacred song and dance. Never suffer any village to be without one while the world endures.

"Through life, as proper people, always worship the Creator. Spend much time dancing, singing, praying, fasting, and observing other rituals.

"If this is done, we will continue to receive abundance from the Good Spirit. The acorn trees shall yield acorns. The rivers shall afford us salmon."

There remained only the "scratching" ceremony. In addition to ears and nasal septum pierced, the *Peheipe* used an obsidian knife to make a "scratch" on the back which drew blood. As each new *Yĕ'poni* knelt down bravely with head forward, the *Peheipe* made the incision. To each new *Yĕ'poni* he announced:

"When you approach the sacred house, say to the doorkeeper, 'I belong to the order. *Ku'ksū* comes before me.'"

It was finished. Deep down inside each initiate it hurt a little, for each knew he had lost his childhood innocence forever.

"You are now *Yĕ'poni!*" the *Peheipe* shouted. With that the ceremony was over. The old members placed their right hands in turn on Tokiwa's left shoulder according to custom. Then they moved on to the next new *Yĕ'poni,* repeating the act until all had been touched.

For ten days following the initiation, Tokiwa and the others again abstained from all meat, and ate nothing but acorn porridge. On the tenth day, the *Peheipe* said, "Go down to the river. Wash yourselves with water. That is good!"

1799

The Falling-Leaf Season

3. Dear Hunting

In Native belief, animals have an intelligence equal to man's.
After all, the animals occupied the earth before man and had
readied the world for humans.

Nisenan Informant

In the Sierra foothills before dawn, Big Meadows,
Nesuya's father, left *Kadema* to hunt deer. Tokiwa and
Yo'to (formerly Pippa) went along. As hunting captain of
Kadema, Big Meadows had the responsiblity to further
direct the new *Yĕ'poni* members in hunting skills and
organization.

"Always find the wind by dropping a handful of dust."
Big Meadows showed the young men. "Always walk into
the wind. This way the game won't catch your scent."

"Be aware of the presence of the animal before he
becomes aware of you. All your senses—sight, hearing,
smell—must be used to gain the advantage. It is your duty
to learn the habits of your prey—to know their nesting
places, the breeding behaviors, and the feeding habits of all
the animals and birds.

"You need also to know their calls. When I want to
attract rabbits until they are only a short distance away

from me, I make this kind of soft kissing sound . . . Pwt!
Pwt! Pwt! (Big Meadows demonstrated on the back of his
hand). To kill rabbits at close range, you want to use a
double pointed arrow. This type of arrow will not pass

(>————←——➤)

completely through his body and disappear into the brush,
and it will stop the rabbit from going down a hole.

"I hate to shoot a rabbit when he runs out, stands, and
puts his ears back and looks right at me. But if he just runs
off it is not so bad."

Big Meadows continued talking as they hiked. "To lay
in ambush for deer, you must get to the crest of a hill where
you can look in all directions. If you see deer, you must go
with stealth, and against the wind."

The three hunters found a hill topped with large
boulders. As the sun came up, they prayed and listened for
the great voice of Nature to tell them what to do. Careless-
ness toward the animal world was severely disapproved of,
for, after all, hadn't the animals occupied the earth before
man?

Soon the hunters heard the noise of crackling leaves.
Deer were grazing on the buckbrush below them. Carefully,
Big Meadows, Tokiwa, and Yo'to disguised themselves
under deerskins and antlered deer heads. They cautiously
moved against the wind concealing themselves behind the
rocks, near where the deer were grazing. Big Meadows
plucked a leaf from a nearby madrone tree and folded it
between his lips. He sucked on it, imitating the whimper of
a fawn. This was certain to bring out a doe, uneasy for the
safety of her young. Bent to the ground, the hunters turned
the antlers, cocking the heads, while simulating the
nibbling of a leaf. These deceptions brought a herd of four
does and one full-grown buck within a few yards of them.

By now the three humans embodied the power of the
deer. Upon receiving a nod from Big Meadows, Tokiwa and

"Maidu Deer Hunters" by Maidu artist Dalbert S. Castro.

Yo'to drew back their bows, a back-up arrow still held in their teeth. As Tokiwa readied his aim, he thought of Big Meadows instructions, "If you aim at the elbow you will shoot straight to the heart. The arrow will go in beneath the elbow."

But just as Tokiwa loosed his first arrow at the buck, the creature dropped its head. The arrow struck with a sudden "Thwack!" atop of its head. Wounded, the deer raised up in surprise. Before it could bolt, Yo'to's first arrow hit the mark. The majestic animal staggered for a short distance before it tumbled onto its side and lay quite still and dead.

The event happened so quickly that the four does remained unsuspecting. They continued to draw in closer, in curiosity, towards the three deer-men. More arrows whizzed at these deer. Before it was over, the hunters succeeded in shooting two of the does.

It was high noon before Big Meadows, Tokiwa, and Yo'to finally finished gutting and skinning the three deer. They carried the larger pieces of meat and hides back to camp. Then they returned for the other usable parts. The deer would provide not only the high protein of the meat, but the back and legs possessed sinewy muscle tendons used to back bows and a variety of other uses. The buckskin hide was used for clothing, earrings, and door coverings. The hooves would be used as rattles. The entire head would be skinned and stuffed with tule material to be used as a hunting decoy. The brain was used to rub over the hides to cure them. Bones and antlers would serve as awls, arrow straighteners, and various other tools.

Walking back to camp with their load of deer meat and skins, Big Meadows told a story. It helped keep their minds off their loads.

"In the beginning when animals could talk, food was plentiful and easy to get," he began. "In order to provide the camp with deer meat, all a man had to do was to go out in the woods and pick up a manzanita stump. If he brought it back in a bag without looking at it along the way, it would have turned into a deer haunch when the sack was finally opened at home. That way, all in the camp shared the meat. Coyote felt hungry for meat one day so he found an enormous stump and started home with it on his back. Halfway home he could contain his hunger no longer so he took out the stump, which he expected to be meat, with the intention of cooking and eating it all himself. The stump had failed to change into meat because of Coyote's wrongdoings, and since then, no one has been able to obtain deer meat in this manner."

Besides the coyote story, every hunter had been instructed in the Nisenan hunting way. He was warned not to eat the game he killed lest he gets worms and brings bad luck upon himself. This taboo meant that as the boys grew in skillfulness with the bow, they would not become independent hunters, rather they would go on to secure meat for their kin, while their own food would be supplied by their relatives. This practice kept kinship ties close.

Back in camp, the people were pleased with the success of the hunters. Big Meadows turned to Tokiwa and Yo'to. "Today you did well. You have moved on from hunting small game to stalking deer. Go again by yourselves and perhaps next year you will both be ready to go with me after bearskins."

Tokiwa and Yo'to were pleased with these words. Bearskins were important for they measured which chief was chief-of-the-region. They, too, wanted to help make Tawec the new chief-of-the-region. But he would have to have the most bearskins. Right now at *Pusuni,* Humpai and Teduwa were the "big chiefs." Together they had many more bearskins brought in by their hunters. Because of this, they could draw upon the surrounding villagers for Big Time celebrations, religious ceremonies, and future community hunts. Tawec, on the other hand, could not draw the neighboring villagers to his place in *Kadema.*

At *Kadema,* Tawec was revered as the best of headmen, otherwise the people would have deposed him without ceremony and installed a new leader. Like all other chiefs, Tawec wore a *makki,* a distinguished headdress, consisting of a straight stick worn at the back of the head and decorated with woodpecker and quail feathers and bits of abalone shell.

Headman Tawec was a natural leader like his father, a chief before him. He had the gift of making everyone cheerful. He was quick and strong and knew the correct thing to do. He was the only adult in *Kadema* who did not have to work and who was allowed to have more than one wife.

With many wives, a chief could develop a large family with more candidates for leadership. This extended family supplied him food and other benefits. He could entertain many visitors, and his wives would do the work to feed and entertain them. If the chief was generous and hospitable to visitors, he acquired a good name, as did the community. He could also lend a wife to another friendly chief, and this also helped to keep the peace.

When the hunters arrived back in *Kadema*, they separated out the deer meat and hides.

"I go to hunt bear in three sleeps," Big Meadows announced. "I will be bear-man that day."

Tokiwa and Yo'to admired the wisdom and courage of their hunting captain. Besides human beings, nothing was more dangerous than the grizzly bear. And being able to embody the power of bear as well as deer were abilities possessed by but a few.

1800

The Ripe Seed Month

4. Grizzly-Man Doctor

"There must be another world when somebody dies or the dead would return."

Jim Dick

In the village of *Yamanködö* Tokiwa and So-se-yah-mah were repairing salmon spears which were kept with the willow twined baskets for catching smaller fish. Soon again it would be the season when the spirit doctor spears the first salmon. This would be an occasion for ceremony. This first salmon would be cooked and all the men would eat a piece. Only then would the fishing begin in earnest.

But now considerable commotion stirred in camp. A runner from downstream had arrived with important news. Tokiwa and his grandfather dropped their work and walked briskly toward the villagers who had encircled the messenger.

"How strange that Ya-hai-lum is not the runner," Tokiwa said to the older man.

They waited patiently for the runner to regain his breath.

"Bad news! Big Meadows, our hunting captain, has been killed by a grizzly bear! It happened near the tule thickets along the river. Bear was first hit with one of Big Meadows' arrows, but Bear then caught hold of our captain and killed him."

When the runner finished telling all the news, two village criers repeated the announcements. Everyone had listened, and now the people began discussing the news in earnest.

Tokiwa quickly turned away after hearing the word. Stunned into a state of denial and isolation, he looked longingly down river towards *Kadema* where Big Meadows lived.

"How can this be?" Tokiwa asked himself. "Big Meadows is the hunting captain. He is as big and strong as a bear himself. He is the very best grizzly-bear man. How can he be dead? He's like my own family... We've hunted together. Nesuya—she and her mother will need my support."

With a cry of anguish, Tokiwa fled. Dragging a log boat from the bank out into the river, he jumped on. He pushed the craft out into swifter water with a long pole and switched to a paddle-blade.

At *Kadema,* he beached his craft on the north side of the river and hurried around the marsh up to the village proper. He heard the awful mourning cry, the ritualized wailing of an entire village. The men wept, but the women mourned the loudest.

"It is true," Tokiwa realized. "Big Meadows *is* dead!" Tears welled up in his eyes as he met two sobbing old women. They stood in the village with their arms outstretched, eyes raised to the sky, in a pleading attitude. He, too, began to cry aloud.

He continued to walk towards Big Meadow's lodge where he found the widow and daughter seated on a large tule mat, their heads covered by rabbit skin blankets. Eyes grief-stricken, they stared off towards the south where Big

Meadows had been killed.

Wypooke had already cut her hair and buried it according to the custom required of mourning widows. She covered her face, arms, legs and breasts with a sticky black pitch made from a mixture of pine resin and burnt black acorn. She would now live in a separate house, attended by an old female relative. She would only leave the house at night and no one was allowed to see her face except the attendant.

Nesuya also covered herself with pitch and would have cut off her long black hair too, but her mother protested vehemently. "No, my daughter," Wypooke whispered. "It is for me to suffer and for you to comfort and support me. Your father knows you grieve enough already in your heart. Only when the "second burning" ceremony is held will I be free with those who also cut their hair."

Nesuya looked up to see Tokiwa's concerned face. He embraced her, comforting her. Releasing her, he turned towards Wypooke and expressed his respect and reassurances toward her with solemn signs.

"We are saddened," Wypooke continued, "but your father's heart travels to *Esto-Yamani*, the big roundhouse of the dead, which lies to the north. It is at *Esto-Yamani* where the soul of all deceased persons lingers four days and then departs to the place in the sky called Heavenly Valley. There his spirit will be greeted by the Earth-Creator, who has a basket of choice food which is always full.

"You know the rest, don't you daughter? Only the spirits of bad people fail to go to heaven. Instead, they remain on earth and enter into the body of a lizard, an owl, a snake, or even a whirlwind. That is why we never hunt or eat lizards, owls, and snakes, and why we fear whirlwinds."

"Mother," Nesuya returned, "Father was never a bad person. This will never happen to him."

"Yes, Nesuya," Wypooke smiled through her tears.

"But your father might 'look back'; he might 'look back' in order to watch and to be close to those like us he dearly loves. If he does 'look back,' he might be turned into a deer or coyote. We had a good man. He was a good husband and father."

As Tokiwa left, he admired Wypooke's courage. But he still hurt. He was angry that Big Meadows had been taken away when he had so many more good years to live. He walked over to some of the men and asked them, "Who was on this bear hunt when Big Meadows got killed? He was a brave and wise hunter. Please tell me what happened!"

"Ya-hai-lum, who is gone, went along on the hunt with Big Meadows," one said. "He is injured, but escaped after having suffered deep cuts on his legs and arms. As a result, we cannot have him in camp for four days because Bear, having tasted his blood, might follow him into camp and injure the women and children and wreck our campground."

Yo'to, Tokiwa's close friend, had also gone on the hunt, but had escaped unhurt. Yo'to saw the sadness in Tokiwa's eyes, and spoke. "I too was with Big Meadows. Our captain showed us where to find bear. They were sleeping inside trees near the tule thickets along the river. Tokiwa, that is where we went and found this bear.

"Do you remember how everyone wanted to make Tawec, our headman, big and rich? We needed to get many bearskins. Just that day of the hunt, Big Meadows had told all of us, 'Our chief will become big and rich by everyone standing together and making each hunter give up bearskins to him. Everyone should help with the hunt. Everyone wants his chief to have a good name. This way we make a big chief.'

"When the killing took place, I was not at the spot. I was looking inside other trees farther down river, so I don't know exactly what happened. But Ya-hai-lum should know."

Four days later, Ya-hai-lum was back visiting the *Kadema* camp. He recounted his story to Tokiwa, but when Ya-hai-lum spoke, there was something about his story that Tokiwa knew didn't sound true.

Tokiwa had thought about a lot of things during those four days. Although not many hunters wanted to hunt grizzly bear, Tokiwa knew that grizzly bearskins were the best for making a chief big and rich. Black bearskins were next in value, and cinnamon bearskins least.

"Big Meadows was a bear doctor who could take on the power of the bear," Tokiwa thought. "He could turn into a grizzly. It was impossible he should die this way."

Tokiwa had observed Big Meadows preparing for the bear hunt many times. First, as captain, he lined the bottom of his quiver with grass and put three poison arrows in, for that was all that custom allowed.

Then he laced himself into the grizzly hide. He adjusted the grizzly's head in such a way that he could open and close the mouth and move the ears. To make claws, he took used dried coffeeberry roots, sharpened until they cut like a knife. He attached these with rawhide to his forearms, so they stuck out beyond the elbows. He tied three or four hollowed-out oak galls underneath each armpit so that when the galls rolled or rattled, they imitated the grizzly's growling. These were some of the preparations he made to turn into a grizzly bear doctor.

Tokiwa listened closely to Ya-hai-lum's account of Big Meadow's death.

"We found a bear-hole, but didn't know what kind of bear was inside," Ya-hai-lum related. "Big Meadows, the grizzly-man, lumbered towards the site. He watched for bear to emerge in the early morning. He checked to see if the wind changed by throwing a handful of dust into the air. He was careful to move so the wind would not carry his scent. He imitated the grizzly's growl, and he nibbled a few berries. Still bear didn't come out.

"We lighted brands to drive the bear from its den. Then

"Big Meadows laced inside grizzly bear hide," by Masaye Hashimoto.

we could shoot it before its eyes adjusted to the light.

"When bear came out, it was a grizzly! I saw Big Meadows' quick release of one arrow which found its mark. This bear was his! The wounded grizzly reared back and roared. Then I saw Big Meadows, under the hide, rear up and roar also.

"As we watched the wounded grizzly, we failed to realize that the wind had suddenly shifted in another direction. I saw the grizzly trying to catch his scent. Our captain edged back to get away from the bear. Suddenly, bear again stood on its hind legs and clawed the air. He had caught the man-smell of our leader!

"Big Meadows was the last to flee. He ran and ran until he could run no more. Then he crawled into a hollow log. The grizzly found him there, pulled him out, and then clawed and crushed him to death.

"This is what I saw happen."

"No! Not good enough, Ya-hai-lum," Tokiwa cried out. "Our captain knew about the wind. But where did *you* stand, Ya-hai-lum?"

Ya-hai-lum's face grew flustered. "Do you doubt my word? That bear almost killed me too! Or do you forget?"

Angrily Tokiwa shouted, "Your word is poison and you're always thinking first of yourself!" He pushed Ya-hai-lum away.

"You snake!" Ya-hai-lum spat. "You are a lame child. It's too bad those *Chucumnes* didn't kill you too, like they did your father."

Ya-ahi-lum then sprang at Tokiwa, thrusting wickedly with his knife. Tokiwa side-stepped his advance, but his foot turned on a round cooking stone. Before he could recover, Ya-hai-lum lunged again. Tokiwa grabbed his knife wrist and they stood there straining, face to face.

Sensing his chance, Tokiwa bent his legs; then fell back, throwing Ya-hai-lum over his head to the ground. Quickly, he whirled and was on his feet, standing over Ya-hai-lum.

Big Matos, who was Big Meadows' brother and had been watching, reached over and took the knife out of Ya-hai-lum's hand and broke up their fight. "Stop this!" he commanded. "This is not an honorable fight. Only one man has a knife. You are both upset about my brother. There must be peace between you two. We will have no more of this."

Tokiwa then shook his fists. "Let us continue fighting but with bare hands," Tokiwa insisted. "That fight will be an even one."

"No! Enough!" Matos repeated, "Calm yourselves. Go and keep to yourselves."

Slowly both young men withdrew.

The villagers prepared for the proper burning of Big Meadows. His body was placed on a bearskin. Headman

Tawec, responsible for the poor and needy, and especially widows, looped strings of beads around the badly mangled body. Mournfully, Wypooke placed one of her prized abalone pendants on her late husband's chest. Tawec provided feather ornaments, food, a pipe, a bow and arrows for Big Meadows' journey. The bearskin was then wrapped close. In this way, he would not need to trouble his living kin.

On the morning after his death, Big Meadow's body and property were burned together so that his spirit could be released and his body could go back to the earth. Tawec directed all this, though he never touched the fire nor the body himself. Those conducting the ceremony used poles to facilitate the burning. Friends and relatives sang and wept and danced about the pyre.

When the body was nearly consumed, Tawec extinguished the fire. He directed the men to carefully scrape up the bones and all the ashes and place them in a new basket. They took these to the village cemetery very close by and raked them into the ground.

Old-Grouse Woman, the medicine women, said she saw a vision of Big Meadows' heart (or soul) exiting from his mouth. "It passed on the wind to the north," she said, "away to the sacred spirit house in *Esto-Yamani*."

Everyone then returned to their homes. That night it began to rain. The skies added their tears to those of the people.

1801

The Acorn-Bread Season

5. The Great Vision

"Do you see the big hill over there?" asked Eagle. "Do you see those three black rocks? That is my camp."

Sison

"It is better to have a burning, for then the widows can be free," Coyote did say.

The curing doctors in *Kadema* announced that the moon fixed by Coyote was fast approaching. Wypooke and the other mourners could wash away the ashes and pitch that covered their bodies. Their hair could grow long again. Widows could remarry. Life would go on. This "second burning" or "cry" ceremony was held once each year. This year it was for Big Meadows and others who had died or been killed in the past twelve months. Some mourners attended three consecutive years.

Invitations were in the form of knotted strings called *puls*. They were sent out by headman Tawec of *Kadema* to five other chiefs, who, in turn, made new *puls* with the necessary number of knots. These were then sent to the leaders of selected families. The *puls* were carried by special runners who were given trespass immunity while on this mission, and were recognized by the single black-and-white gull feather they wore.

For this occasion, each *pul* had twenty knots, which meant there were twenty intervening days before the ceremony commenced. The recipient cut off a knot with each new sunrise until the time arrived for departure to *Kadema.* So-se-yah-mah had received a *pul* on behalf of Tokiwa's household and all made preparations to attend.

But other things were happening in Tokiwa's life. Over the year, Tokiwa had devoted much of his energies to courting Nesuya. Alone in the forest, they held secret meetings. They promised to marry soon. In the evenings under the moonlight, they risked discovery by such romantic trysts. They knew that if, for some reason, the old people should catch them, the elders could order a doctor to kill them both. It happened to others before.

The old ones cautioned the unmarried girls especially to behave, saying: "You must not go sleeping with all and sundry any more. The doctors will kill you if you are flighty! Nobody is going to marry you if you are flighty. The doctors won't let you live long!

"Marriage is sacred. You must keep your honor and be responsible to your partner. If not, divorce is simple. Either you or your husband may pick up and leave. The man can end things by walking out and leaving all his belongings behind. You simply return to your parents.

"You must never be adulterous. This is the most damaging thing that either party can do to break up a marriage. Either party may kill the lover on the spot, or even worse, kill the lover's best friend so he or she will have to live with that knowledge the rest of his life. There is no punishment for killings such as these."

One night, when Tokiwa was old enough, So-se-yah-mah spoke to him about marriage. He said, "Grandson, you must let the old people agree to your marriage, so the marriage will be good. Then the couple lives long, and there is group harmony with their friends and family. Show the girl's family that you are a good hunter. Let the girl show our family that she will do her work."

So Tokiwa brought meat to his prospective mother-in-law to prove that his hunting ability was good. Nesuya, on the other hand, brought acorn flour to Tokiwa's family in *Yamanködö* to prove she was not lazy. This both lovers continued for one year. Not until then did the elders begin to have *wenne hon,* "good feelings," about the marriage.

Nesuya reminded Tokiwa that even before Big Meadows' death, her mother's behavior towards him had changed significantly. Wypooke no longer conversed directly with Tokiwa nor looked at him. A strict taboo between mother-in-law and son-in-law prevailed. If Wypooke met Tokiwa along the footpaths, she would pull a deerskin over her head and face. This was taken as a positive sign that Wypooke approved their marriage.

All this had happened by the time of the "cry" ceremony. The last knots on the *puls* were about to be cut. When the sun showed pink in the western sky, the guests, loaded with baskets of food and gifts, began converging on *Kadema.* Most of the visitors had traveled since early morning. They arrived with weapons, the men in front; the women behind. They brought with them long willow poles upon which the objects to be burned are suspended; the gifts to the dead.

Headman Tawec, along with his two wives, welcomed the guests into camp. *Wöo,* the Secret Society's crier, under orders of the *Peheipe,* sat on top of the *kúm* and called to the people, "Be alert and have no quarrels. There are no enemies. Everyone is a friend. Be well-behaved men and women. Come along and go right inside." He finished these admonitions with a friendly, *"He iiiii!"*

The people came to camp to be close to the graves of those relatives who had died in the last year. The spirits would return to visit and would be watching. Property would be burned as offerings to these spirits of the dead. In return, the spirits would protect the people from all spiritual and material terrors. The property would be set on the long poles, like flags, to be broken and thrown into the fire along with articles the dead had held. The poles would bear fish, deer meat, clothes, and new baskets. Fish nets, wild iris cordage, and all kinds of food would be added. Mourners would wail and cry night-long and finally the widows would be free.

Then, the next day a celebration with the trading of gifts between hosts and guests, feasting, gambling, foot ball and foot races, and more games would follow. The trading would do much to strengthen family ties and provide opportunities for the exchange of material goods. Also, the widows would pay for a string necklace made of beads, furs, and food. At the end of five years, by custom, these necklaces would be returned.

Tawec saw that the visiting groups were fed. Then the clowns came out of the dance house and yelled, "People, tie up your property. The burning time has arrived."

Guests and relatives, using milkweed twine, tied their presents of baskets, pieces of clothing, and food onto the poles and walked together to the cemetery ground close by. They uncovered human ashes and stacked wood directly over the graves. Tawec directed the pyre be lit, making a great fire. A brush wall surrounded the pyre within which the dancers and mourners performed in a circle, holding their offerings.

All that night there was wailing and crying.

Now Old-Grouse Woman, the respected doctor at *Kadema*, had been requested by headman Tawec to cast the extremely sacred "image" of Big Meadows into the fire. She had prepared the image for Big Meadows, for he was a member of the Secret Society and was entitled to have one placed with him at his death. Old-Grouse Woman forbade gambling or hand clapping during the dedication. To insult the image meant death.

The effigy looked like a doll, made from wildcat skin and stuffed with tule. She had added eyes made of abalone, and she had directed that the image be carried over hills and through valleys where Big Meadows had traveled during his life, for it contained his spirit, *ku-kini-busdi.*

The presence of the image at the ceremony now recalled the memory of Big Meadows and filled the mourners with piercing sorrow. The image marked the peak of the ceremony. The people wailed and cried in a frenzy. They shouted in elation, celebration and joy. One by one, the men pulled a pole from the ground. They took all the property on the pole and cast it into the fire. Then they cast the poles into the fire. Now the image was cast in. This was very good! The people's year-long religious obligations had been met, and so, the widows were free. But more significantly, the ghosts or souls of the deceased could be seen dancing slowly around the fire. The people watched them dance!

The next day, the participants engaged in celebrations. They gambled and feasted. Two *Peheipes* went out among the oaks to dress. They covered themselves with white paint and tied moth cocoon rattles on their ankles. These *Peheipes,* the tribal clowns whose role it was to also be ridiculous as Coyote, did many annoying tricks. They walked over people, walked between them when they were talking, and came too close to others. When they saw people eating, they stole their food. The clowns kept on acting in an obnoxious manner, provoking and teasing.

Now it was the second evening. Everyone crowded inside the dance house, for Old-Grouse Woman would "spirit-talk." Upon entering every person circled in counterclockwise fashion around the entire dance floor. They placed a gift by the spirit pole and then sat down on the soft pine needles, the men on one side and the women on the opposite side. This night the people completely filled the *kúm*, with very little space remaining for the dancers. In preparation for the spirit-meeting, ribbons of feathers were placed on the spirit pole, for spirits would come in and travel down this pole.

Old-Grouse Woman was both a sucking doctor and a dream doctor, for she had the ability to cure and to cause disease with *ca'win* or "poison," and she had the gift of "spirit-talking." She would speak aloud in the voices of the spirits. She could recall the past and predict the future. She could conjure up spirits and voices of the deceased. She could make herself invisible, and, through trances, teleport herself to other places. Her world was a place where every object was endowed with potential supernatural powers.

She was the most patient of doctors. She had a good heart. But many feared her because they knew women doctors were more likely to use poison. Old-Grouse Woman had knowledge of secret poisons because the spirit world was known to her. She knew how to shoot a person with *sila* or "poison sticks." Sometimes she would infect others with illness by throwing physical pain long distances. She demonstrated the proper method of throwing the invisible pains by blowing them from her extended palm. She could procure the *ca'win* used to kill people readily from the air, the water, or from the ground.

Old-Grouse Woman was so old no one knew her age. The people believed she had lived at the time before there were humans. She told the people to behave themselves and be good. "Otherwise," she warned, "that tree over there, or the wind, could kill you if it wanted to." She reminded everyone to make extra acorn bread and to prepare plenty of gifts for the second burning ceremony to help insure that only good events would happen in the months ahead. She had such power that everything she prophesied happened.

With everyone seated, the singers entered the *kúm* first, followed by Tokiwa and the other *Yĕ'poni* dancers and finally the women dancers. The sound of the *wadada*, the elderberry clapper sticks, and the large *dul*, the great foot drum accompanied the dancers who danced to gain power. They knew they would lose power and the world would not stay balanced if they did not dance.

So-se-yah-mah, as dance captain, directed the sacred dances. Each dance was divided into four parts and four rounds or repetitions made up one part. All male performers painted red, white, and black stripes on their bodies and legs and vertical stripes on their faces. Each man wore a *wolza*, a feather headdress, together with a salmon-orange flicker feather headband that hung down on his brow covering the eyes, and stuck out about six inches on either side. Each man also wore a back apron, and a breech-cloth. They carried several whistles called *tokas* made of prairie falcon bones, which they blew continuously as they danced. The best dancer performed with his mouth filled with whistles, all pitched on the same key. He gave forth intermittent whistle blasts by alternating sucking and blowing of his breath.

The women wore beautiful deerskin dresses, heavily decorated with beads and shell ornaments which clicked melodiously as they moved. Nesuya's belt was made of red-colored woodpecker scalps and green mallard duck feathers framed with tiny white shell beads.

The men danced in step holding their hands in front of them, palms down, bent forward at the waist, legs apart, and heads moving from side to side, causing the flicker headbands to swing to and fro at the same time.

The women danced in place, alternatingly raising and

"Tulej Dance" by Maidu artist Dalbert S. Castro.

lowering their right and left hands, while holding their
elbows near their sides. They carried the sacred wormwood
herb, kept burning inside a short hollow root tube with a
live coal inserted inside. The aromatic smoke wafted
throughout the dance house, as a measure to ward off
sickness and evil spirits. The fire cast tall shadows of the
dancers upon the walls.

When the performers finished and the singing and
sounds of *wadada, dul* and *tokas* subsided, they went
outside and ate an acorn soup meal together. Custom
prohibited a dancer from eating by himself at such a time
for fear of becoming sick.

Old-Grouse Woman now began singing and shaking
the most sacred *wososo,* a cocoon rattle, at the bottom of the
spirit post. The people returned back inside. The rattle
began its "spirit talking." Immediately everyone fell silent.
Darkness shrouded all as the fire was reduced to coals by
the *Peheipe* so that the spirits of the dead might appear.

In the silence of the impenetrable darkness, Nesuya wished for the security of Tokiwa's arms. They sat across from each other, shivering with excitement.

Then the *wososo* rattle sounded in a low, ominous quivering close to the ground, much like a rattlesnake's sound. The rattle seemed to travel up the spirit post, slowly first and then gaining momentum. Finally it shot up all at once, and seemed to dart about the top of the room with amazing speed, giving forth terrific rattles and low, buzzing quavers, now and then banging up against the spirit post with a thud.

Then a roaring sound was heard outside. It was a spirit! Old-Grouse Woman lay down and had stopped shaking the rattle. The people sat quietly, straining to hear more.

"Tsh-Tsh-Tsh-Tsh! Tsh-Tsh-Tsh-Tsh! Tsh-Tsh-Tsh-Tsh! Tsh-Tsh-Tsh-Tsh!" Ghost spirits had taken up the rattle and were shaking it! A ghost was a disembodied apparition of the dead. Sometimes they would cry, sometimes sing, sometimes tell of the cause or circumstances of their death. These ghost spirits were known to the audience because they named themselves. People who wished might touch them: They had no head or limbs but were as smooth as a thigh. Sometimes a ghost spirit would not let go of the rattle; then Old-Grouse Woman blew tobacco on it and the rattle could be heard to fall as the ghost spirit departed.

One spirit arrived, picked up the rattle, shook it a little and began mumbling through the body of Old-Grouse Woman. The people listened expectantly, for the old doctor was able to talk directly with spirits whenever she sought advice for the people. They heard the spirit say, "One of the men here tonight will be a *yo-mi,* a medicine doctor. He can hear everything along *No'to-mom,* for he lives close to the water baby, *Unai.*"

Tokiwa, sitting up front, heard the words and his heart

pounded with excitement. He knew that the spirit, talking through Old-Grouse Woman's lips, was talking about him. He was one of the few present who lived at *Yamanködö* and who had heard the high mewing call of *Unai.* Too, he had been giving thought to becoming a doctor.

Inside the pitch-black dance house, the discourse was temporarily disrupted when the coyote spirit came inside. The people recognized it by its howling from far off. Everyone inside made a special sound with their mouths, blowing vociferously, and driving off the coyote spirit to the relief of the people.

The séance resumed as the first spirit returned. It foretold of good acorn harvests, the plant-foods which would do poorly, and which hunts would go well in the months ahead. The spirit then lowered its voice to add:

"This man here tonight who will be a *yo-mi,* I see he was a close brother to Big Meadows. The two were very close.

"I see this man traveling alone to *Esto-Yamani,* spirit mountain. He goes there because Big Meadows has a whispering to tell this *yo-mi* before he passes on again to the place in the sky."

The rattle dropped to the ground as the spirit departed. The *Peheipe* quickly raked open the fire and threw in pitch-pine, straw, and kindling. As the blaze sprang up, the *kúm* filled with strong light. Old-Grouse Woman slowly got to her feet. The drummer resumed stamping on the log foot drum. People began singing. Others began talking about what had just happened.

Tokiwa found himself outside in the starlight without at first realizing where he was. He could see *O-to,* the seven stars in the heavens. He began to shiver both from the excitement and from the cold. Later that night, as Tokiwa slept in the smaller guest lodge, he dreamed.

Tokiwa saw Big Meadows' face again clearly, looking at him from white vapor clouds. He smiled at Tokiwa. Then Tokiwa saw Old-Grouse Woman's face with eyes that shone fire-red like the sun. She, too, floated in churning white clouds. In definite tones, Old-Grouse Woman repeated her words, "The person who loves Big Meadows is before me. He, who has this knowledge to be a doctor for his people, goes to Spirit Mountain. He listens to Eagle, the immortal one, the Everlasting Spirit, the Good Spirit who gives the people plenty of *ooti,* acorns."

The dream shifted. Tokiwa saw a great eagle. The eagle flew round and round downward alighting near him.

"What are you doing here?" the eagle asked.

"I am just lying down," said Tokiwa.

"When you are joy-walking you should go to my house," said Eagle.

"Where is your camp?" asked Tokiwa.

"Do you see the big hill over there? Do you see those three black rocks? There is my camp."

"How many days will it take me to go there?"

"You can get there in seven days."

"I will go tomorrow," said Tokiwa.

In his dream, Tokiwa left in the morning and traveled for seven days. When he got to the foot of the mountain, he saw a spring of water. Consumed with thirst, he drank and drank. Then he tumbled over, his belly swollen with water.

Eagle, missing him, went to look for him and found him. He alighted near him. He said, "Get on my back, I will take you."

They flew to the eagle's camp on the mountain top. "Are you hungry?" the eagle asked.

"Yes, Tokiwa responded.

"Don't be afraid," the eagle assured. "Kick that rock three times and say 'Open!' and go in."

Tokiwa did so and the rock opened.

Two panthers held their heads together across the opening as if to catch him. But he entered without being afraid. Then he saw two horned creatures who threatened to gore him. He continued without fear. Flames jumped back and forth across the doorway, yet Tokiwa walked between the flames without fear.

As he dreamed, Tokiwa saw many Indians singing and dancing. One looked very familiar to Tokiwa. Eagle said, "Feed him!" so the people gave him food. He remained there for three days.

Eagle then advised, "Kick the other rock three times and say "Open!" It opened. "Do you see that fork in the road? When you come to the left-hand road, you must go that way. An enemy is watching on the right hand road. Then go to the lake."

Tokiwa followed the path and when he came to the fork in the road, he took the left hand road, which led him to a lake. As he walked along the bank of the lake, a young woman came out from behind a black willow bush. She ran into the water until she was waist deep. Then she stood there.

"Where are you going?" she asked.

"I am going to the north country," he said.

"The sun is almost down. Please go to my house!" she implored. "If you kick that rock three times it will open. You must stay there for I will come in the night."

Tokiwa obeyed, went in and stayed. In the night, the young woman came. She gave him a hair ring to wear on his finger. That kept Tokiwa.

Tokiwa woke up from his dream. He wanted to rush to Nesuya and tell her of the dream, but she and Wypooke were still sleeping. It would be wrong to go into their lodge.

He would tell his family all that had happened. So-se-yah-mah, especially, would be told. He would interpret the dream so Tokiwa rushed to see him.

As he walked along the foot trail that morning, the new day was crisp and bright, the sky a clear blue. The cotton-wood trees along the river had turned a fiery golden-yellow. Tokiwa saw quail and rabbits. He heard the crested wood-pecker in the tall oaks and the beavers and turtles splashing along the river. He sensed that the earth, the water, the sky, the plants and animals, and the people were all one.

Occasionally, Tokiwa stopped to listen that he might hear the voice of *Unai*, the water spirit. His thoughts turned to the creation story and to Spirit Mountain. He climbed the tallest tree to catch a glimpse of the sacred mountain some distance to the north. He could not quite see it. He knew it to be the sacred place where a person's inner heart goes at death, where the spirit rests, washes its face at the springs, and then sets out for Heavenly Valley, following the Milky Way.

As Tokiwa continued on, he suddenly shuddered. "Is that a spirit touching me?" he wondered. "There is a purpose for everything. Big Meadows had returned!" Tokiwa could sense he was very close and was comforted.

1801

The Acorn-Bread Season

6. Journey to Esto-Yamani

"The Sky is our roof, The Earth, our floor.
We follow the smoking trail,
To the World beyond the smokehole."

Coyote Man

When Tokiwa was back home in *Yamanködö*, he discussed the strange séance and vivid dream with So-se-yah-mah and the others. The elders paid serious attention to what was being said, for dreams were an important aspect to their way of life.

"You must understand, my grandson, that dreaming does not take place entirely within your being. Rather, dreaming is a way of communication superior to ordinary seeing or hearing. In dreams you come into close contact with the spirit world through the spirit helpers."

After listening, Tokiwa and the elders nodded their heads.

So-se-yah-mah continued, "Grandson, your séance and dream are powerful, for to dream of a dead person is to be visited by a ghost. But you must only listen, for if you speak to a ghost, then in that moment you will die."

So-se-yah-mah gestured towards Tokiwa and extended his arms skyward, "My grandson is called to Spirit Mountain to gain power to be a doctor. For this he must prepare well, for the spirits watch for wrongdoings. They watch from the mountains, *Tuj-ma Ole Jamin* and *Esto-Yamani.*"

"Then to which spirit mountain must I go?" Tokiwa asked perplexed.

"In her vision, did not Old-Grouse Woman see Big Meadows' shadow travel north with the wind at the time of his burning?" So-se-yah-mah asked. "And is not the *Esto-Yamani* in that same direction?"

Grandfather continued, "Grandson, you are not a doctor naturally endowed with power, nor have you inherited it as some do. But you do possess the heart to seek it out. Remember, sometimes power itself seeks people out. It is right that you go to *Esto-Yamani* and seek knowledge for yourself."

"But I fear the ghosts," Tokiwa protested.

"So do I," laughed Grandfather softly.

So-se-yah-mah stood up and beat his chest, in order to talk to God. Praying aloud, he asked:

"*Aikat,* Creator, invisible Good and Great Spirit, you who constantly watch over and befriend us who still live on earth, give courage and safety to Tokiwa, my grandson, who will soon journey to pray before your spirit house amongst the three black rocks.

"He journeys to seek knowledge and to be close to Big Meadows' heart which has returned up the ladder from the sky.

"Great Spirit, grant Tokiwa your spiritual power so that he may lead a life of caring for others; that he may become a great doctor for our people some day."

Although Tokiwa still felt wary, he accepted his grandfather's pronouncements. He could never question a family elder who spoke out in public, for this would disgrace the entire family.

Tokiwa stood up and raised his hand, thereby declaring that he accepted all of what had been said. When the elders saw this, they shouted "Ho!" in agreement. Everyone prepared to help Tokiwa make ready for his holy pilgrimage.

Esto-Yamani, to the north, meant literally "the middle hills" or "mountain set-in-the-center." It was a holy place to the Maidu-Nisenan groups. The creation story taught the people that *Aikat*, the Creator, kept his *Ku'kinim Kumi*, spirit house, there. After the world had been created, *Aikat* stood upon its highest peak and made camp. Just to the north he made the first man named *Ku'ksū* and the first woman named *Banakam Mo-lo-Kyle*, Morning Star Woman.

The Buttes marked a "stopping place" of the Creator. Therefore, they were forever rich in spiritual power called *pe* (pā). Gaining *pe* provided many benefits, so pilgrimages were frequently made. *Pe* provided good gambling medicine. *Yo-mi* could obtain help in divining events through prolonged dreamwork. *Pe* could also help ensure greater contact with the spirit world by conjuring up spirits and voices of the dead.

At the same time, there were the ghosts which Tokiwa feared, where the dead lingered four days before departing to Heavenly Valley, the special place in the sky. "When you leave this earth," the elders taught, "you leave through *Esto-Yamani*. Ghosts are always present, and blow about constantly crying."

Many times in his boyhood, Tokiwa had seen this queer mountain range rising in dramatic isolation from the wide floor of the valley. Every spring he went with his mother, Woyectena, and a small party from their village, to help gather clover, grass seeds, roots, bulbs, and earthworms, often staying for weeks. The fireflowers, and golden poppies spread a shimmering fire mantle over the valley floor. Sky-blue lupine was also in blossom. Still, some of the

The Sutter Buttes landscape. Photograph by Robert Burrill.

elders refused to travel this country or camp anywhere close to the hills because they respected the presence of ghosts.

Tokiwa remembered the Buttes as consisting of a series of low rounded, gray-green colored hills. South Butte, the tallest, most resembled the large assembly-house of Maidu-Nisenan history. Though the Buttes and the marsh lands around them were unsettled and unowned, they were hunted and fished in by all Indian groups who lived in the vicinity.

Tokiwa remembered how, at every sunrise, noon, and again at sunset, his party would stop to face the Buttes and offer prayers of thankfulness, and to commune in meditation with the Supreme Being.

Each time Tokiwa experienced an eerie, uncanny

feeling as he looked at the Buttes during the daytime or at night. *Esto-Yamani* was more than a mountain range! In the daytime, Tokiwa and his people could see filmy vapors of what looked like smoke, rising up out of the mountain. Yet, there was no one camping by the Buttes to suggest they were seeing campfire smoke. What *were* those vapors, then?

At night, mysterious lights were noticed in the hills, stirring the elders to recount the ancient legends about *Esto Yamani*.

One such story passed down by an informant from ancient times was that the elders saw the lights from fires of spirit campers or ghosts on the Buttes. Hence, the people were afraid to go in there because of the *Ka'Kinim* spirits.

"Grandson, all things in life involve some risk. You will be with the *Yĕ'poni* elders in *Molokúm* once you reach the Buttes. You shall be safe."

Tokiwa was somewhat reassured, but still apprehensive

South Butte is the highest, standing at 2,132 feet, and most resembles an Indian spirit house. Photo by Robert Burrill.

of what he might encounter. The elders made preparations for Tokiwa's journey. Grandfather took Tokiwa into the sweatlodge for special instructions, meditation, and one final cleansing. Again, Tokiwa fasted. He ate only unsalted acorn soups and bread, as the doctors prescribed. He received a special *we-da*, an amulet, consisting of a section of angelica root worn as a pendant, for it would provide trespass immunity and tell all he met that his mission was of a religious nature.

Tokiwa's journey to Spirit Mountain must take seven days, for this was how it happened in his dream. His destination was near the Buttes, a village called *Molokúm*, or "Morning-Star dance house," built to honor the first woman of creation. Once there, he would partake in the proper rites for spirit contact.

With the support of the larger group, Tokiwa left. To stay warm, he wore an otter skin cape over his shoulders. He placed his bow, and otter-skin quiver filled with arrows, high over his right shoulder. He carried his bobcat-skin travel pouch filled with beads, acorn cakes, a dry buckeye fire stick and cedar hearth, an obsidian knife, fishhooks, and cordage. A grizzly bearskin, which belonged to So-se-yah-mah, would be his gift to the headman of *Molokúm*. So-se-yah-mah carefully rolled it up and tied it upon Tokiwa's shoulders.

Tokiwa headed downstream following the well-established foot trails that led from village to village. These followed stream drainages, and led to crossings. Tokiwa would pass through *Kadema* first and then travel to the larger village complex of *Pusuni* located at the mouth of the *No'to-mom*. Then he would head north along the Big North Water River and pass through *Totola, Wishuna, Leuchi,* and *Wollock*, all Nisenan villages. At *Wollock*, Tokiwa would cross the *Káyimceu* River, which entered there and follow it north, traveling through *Olo, Yukulme, Hok, Sisum,* and

Mimal before finally reaching *Molokúm.*

Tokiwa stopped at *Kadema* and saw Wypooke no longer in mourning for the first time in over a year. Her face was washed clean and her hair would grow long, and she wore beautiful clothes again.

Nesuya prepared a good meal for Tokiwa. She had just returned from gathering angleworms, accomplished by thrusting a stick into the wet ground and moving it in a rotary motion. The oily creatures crawled to the surface where she gathered them into baskets. She then boiled them in water, causing the worm oil to rise to the surface, which she then eagerly skimmed off for food. In addition to this delicacy, Nesuya served succulent freshwater clams and acorn soup flavored with powdered grasshoppers.

Unfortunately, Tokiwa had to fast. He told Nesuya that he could only eat plain acorn mush.

With her back to Tokiwa and face covered, Wypooke asked Nesuya, "Why will he not eat?"

Tokiwa explained, "Nesuya, I go to Spirit Mountain, the middle-hills. I have heard the spirits say that Big Meadows has whisperings there to tell me. I also had a powerful dream in which your father's ghost spoke to me."

Nesuya's heart became glad, "I will help you Tokiwa," she said. She added more acorn cakes to his food pouch. Through Nesuya, Wypooke, who had heard everything, wished Tokiwa "*Citapai o mie*—to take care of himself and farewell."

He spent the first night, uneventfully, at *Pusuni,* where he visited the two headmen brothers, Humpai and Teduwa. Teduwa reassured him, "Spirit Mountain is some distance to the north, up the Big North Water River."

"Behind those trees in the morning," Humpai pointed, "there are places from which you can see Spirit Mountain. But ghosts live there and we won't travel there ourselves."

They added little more. For now, they were more

concerned that the Big North Water River might flood this year, as it had the rainy season before.

Early next morning, after breakfasting on more acorn soup, Tokiwa headed north. Much of the area on this side of the river was still heavy with tule growth. The sacred mountain could not be seen. There had not been any fire drives yet this fall to burn off the underbrush. The marshy tule reeds were higher than a man could reach. But the trail was well-established from heavy use.

As he walked, he saw many more animals than people. He realized the truth of the elders' words that the Creator first made earth in the world, then plants, then animals, and then human beings. Tokiwa saw large herds of tule elk, a favorite food source of the grizzly bear. Fortunately, the grizzlies he saw were across the river from him.

Tokiwa observed the antelope, beaver, and otter. Sturgeon, trout, steelhead, and salmon teemed in the rivers. In some places, the salmon turned the waters silvery because they migrated upstream in such great numbers.

The skies above were filled with the flights of thousands of waterfowl—large honker geese, green necked mallard ducks, white-backed and long-tailed ducks and many others. Pairs of red-headed cranes and pure white egrets ignored Tokiwa's approaching footfalls until he was almost on top of them.

The foot trail took Tokiwa to the ferry one mile upstream from the mouth of the *Káyimceu*. There, an elderly Nisenan ferryman waited to take passengers across on his log raft boat. His boat consisted of two logs, lashed with grapevine. The logs were made plank-like on the side intended for the deck; and the ends rose slightly up into a prow and stern.

The ferryman provided his service and expected to be paid only what his passengers offered. This ferryman covered his face so no one ever saw it. He stood silently, his head thrust forward in concentrated thought.

"Who is this ferryman?" Tokiwa thought, "Why do I feel uneasy?"

Only after stepping ashore and walking a considerable distance, did Tokiwa realize that he had forgotten to pay the ferryman any fee, nor had the ferryman asked. Tokiwa quickly retraced his steps, but the boat and ferryman were gone. Perplexed, he resumed his journey.

He passed through *Yukulme* and spent the night at *Hok.* Here Tokiwa first saw the Buttes up close. The mountain range loomed above mid-morning fog. His destination was close at hand.

Here, also, Tokiwa came to realize that he was entering another language area wherein his Nisenan dialect was more and more replaced by the Konkow Maidu dialect. Tokiwa discovered that the people at *Hok* used the word *yandih* instead of *kúm* to denote "house." Indeed, *yandih* could be used interchangeably to mean "house" or "mountain." This makes sense, Tokiwa thought, for the closest mountain in the area also contains the sacred spirit house.

The people at *Hok* were dutifully supportive of Tokiwa's religious mission, as had been all the others with whom he had met and stayed. Every village headman saw that he received food, lodging, and plenty of firewood for warmth at night.

Tokiwa counted out the seventh of the shells that he carried, which told him how many days had passed since he had left home. *Molokúm* was only a little distance more. Never before had Tokiwa been so close to the Buttes. He stopped and said a prayer of thankfulness that his journey had been safe. He prayed that the doctors at *Molokúm* would help him.

The rest of the trip to *Molokúm* continued without problems. *Molokúm* rested on a high mound close to the

View of the Nisenan village of Yupu in 1852, near Yuba City with Sutter Buttes in background. Depicted are acorn granaries and large dome-shaped, earth-covered dwellings. Courtesy of the R.H. Lowie Museum of Anthropology, University of California, Berkeley.

mouth of the Yuba River. When the rain waters came to this area, the Buttes would be surrounded by a great lake. The winds that blew across it caused the waters to look like the vast ocean far to the west.

The rainy season, about to begin, was the time when the animals and birds sought refuge among the three largest black buttes. Here, all the creatures found shelter, food, and protection.

Ahead Tokiwa saw steam and smoke columns rising above the willow trees. It was *Molokúm!* He was quick to notice the round dance-house which crowned the mound in the center of the village. "It is so large!" Tokiwa exclaimed. "At least twice the size of either of the two dance houses at *Kadema.*"

The people decorated this great dance house handsomely with bearskins which hung from the roof, adding streamers and festoons of different lengths. Some of the streamers were twelve feet long, made entirely of flicker feathers!

Besides the dance house, *Molokúm* consisted of over

twenty-five dome-shaped smoke-blackened lodges. Women and children were busy at work and play. Near each lodge stood one, sometimes two, acorn granaries of wicker-work mounted on posts as high as one's head and capped with thatch material. Many were filled with freshly-gathered acorns.

As Tokiwa walked closer, he found he was no stranger to the crowd he saw before him. Runners had passed on ahead, telling who he was, from whence he came, and the nature of his mission.

On top of the great dance house stood a *Peheipe* who proclaimed Tokiwa's arrival to everyone. *"Wenne He iiiii!* good medicine," he called loudly, *"Wenne He iiiii!"*

In front of the west door of the dance house stood many doctors. They wore beautiful white and grey goose feather robes. Around their necks each doctor wore a large abalone gorget and other jewelry. Since it was tribal propriety, when receiving guests, to wait two or three hours in silence before addressing one another, all reclined and quietly smoked their tobacco, according Tokiwa the same privilege. In time, servings of warm acorn-porridge were passed around.

For a long time, the silence continued. Only occasionally did the doctors glance at their guest.

Tokiwa grew impatient. "What is it with these people? Will we ever speak?" he wondered.

Suddenly something jumped down off the roof and landed just behind Tokiwa. It was the *Peheipe* and he shouted, *"He iiiii! He iiiii!"* into Tokiwa's ears. Instinctively, Tokiwa had reacted by jumping back and rolling away in the dust. Everyone laughed except Tokiwa, who was frightened. But before he had a chance to recover, the clown continued to taunt Tokiwa, advancing so close, their eyes were just fingers apart.

The clown stood with his head tilted, displaying a

toothless, comical expression, and a strange look in his eyes. Tokiwa felt he was witnessing the primordial Coyote himself. He wore a garish red and white "line and dot" paint pattern that crossed one side of his face and then continued down both arms and legs. He wore a large top-knot head-dress, made of black feathers.

This clown was not only outlandish, his antics seemed ridiculous. Lying on his stomach now, he made blubbering, gurgling sounds with his hands to his mouth. Tokiwa began laughing with the others. Then the clown rose, half-leaped, tripped himself, and fell noisely to the ground again in a pile of dust. Picking himself up, he ran away, disappearing inside the low arched entrance of the assembly/dance house. Everyone made cat-calls and shouts of approval.

Now two venerable, silver-haired priests—curing doctors—approached Tokiwa. Their names were Owa and Hoo-du-sa. They wore feathered headdresses and long mantles of eagle's feathers that reached below their knees.

Tokiwa stood and presented the doctor-chiefs with the prized grizzly bear hide. When it was rolled open, two other doctors hurried over and immediately stroked the bearskin several times with stalks of wormwood to "calm the bear down," for they knew that bears had been human beings before the present race of Indians. They stroked a bearskin so its spirit might not be angered. Bundles of wormwood were tied onto the hide and then the doctors went back to meditating and lying on their backs to smoke their stone pipes.

Tokiwa's gift, the prized grizzly bear hide, had been a superior gift, the doctors told him. He felt relieved and pleased. The men escorted Tokiwa to the doorkeeper of the dance house, while a distant drummer inside kept time by stamping with his feet on the hollow slab-foot drum. The *Ku'ksū hesi* dance was about to begin.

The door was made low so that it was necessary to stoop over in passing through. As each man entered, he bent low to crawl down through the entrance way, sometimes backing through slowly. Each person recited four times to the doorkeeper: "I belong to the Order. *Ku'ksū* comes before me."

When Tokiwa's turn came, he showed his scarred back and also displayed his angelica root amulet, as he stated four times, "I belong to the Order. *Ku'ksū* comes before me."

The doorkeeper allowed his entry.

But upon walking through the doorway, the *Peheipe* came running, asking everyone to be silent. "Listen! Everybody listen! Can you hear it?"

Everyone listened, and Tokiwa watched as everyone's face grew somber and grave. Yes, there was a strange noise all right. Tokiwa heard an errie, pulsating kind of roaring sound, which grew louder. "Whoo r... whoo r... whoo r," it sounded.

It was coming from outside the dance house, down behind the mound perhaps. Tokiwa ventured outside behind the *Peheipe* to take a second look. The roaring sound grew louder still. Tokiwa's heart pounded faster and his palms sweated.

What he now saw was extraordinary—a completely feathered *Ku'ksū* spirit was slowly moving towards him, accompanied by escorts! The spirit dancer had his face and body blackened to be unrecognizable and dressed in a great crow and raven cloak, called the *moki,* which along with a tall, thick set of hawk-wing feathers, fit into a netted cap covering his head and face. The topmost central feather of the headdress was a large bald eagle's wing feather painted white with chalk. There were also four long flicker feather headbands that reached from the shoulders all the way down to the knees!

In cadence and in single file, the procession advanced

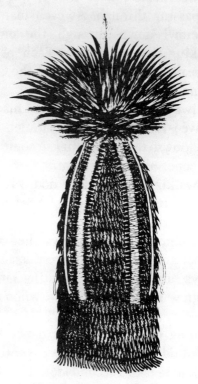

Ku'ksŭ moki dance regalia.

with the feathered body made red by the setting sun. In front and on both sides of the *moki* dressed spirit walked young initiate escorts, two of whom were each whirling a bull-roarer, a long thong, which in turn, was tied to a slat of wood. The slats, when whirled in the air, made the humming, pulsating noise. Tokiwa knew that the bull-roarers were played to clear the air prior to dancing and singing and as a caution to passersby. Should a person be touched by any of the *moki* cloak feathers, that one would become sick. Tokiwa knew of two people who had touched such feathers. They got chills and fever, and would have died had they not been doctored right away. Several innocent villagers threw themselves onto the ground, their hands covering their eyes.

It appeared to Tokiwa that the feathered *Ku'ksū* dancer had his backside to him. At any moment the dancer might end his hiding by turning around and revealing his god-face to him. Thinking this, Tokiwa thought of the creation story and how Coyote alone could see the Earth-Maker's face. The powerful feathers hung suspended throughout, swaying with the slightest movement of the wearer. The sight of this ghostly creature was terrifying to children, and frightening to adults.

In short order, Tokiwa decided to retreat inside the dance house before the parade came too close. He sensed that their entire presence was unworldly. Somehow the *Ku'ksū*-god, *Aikat*, depicted by the elaborate wardrobe of feathers, was actually present within the performer.

Back inside, all the men sat anxiously waiting. Tokiwa was given the seat of honor, the chief's seat, farthest inside from the door and just to the right of the foot drum. Several other Secret Society dancers were present as well, ornamented with all their wealth of feathers.

As dusk approached, pitch-pine sticks were ignited to help illuminate the interior. A pair of *yok'-koli* garlands that encircled the interior of the dance house could be better seen. The upper *yok'-koli* hung at head level. It consisted of many kinds of acorns, alternating at short intervals with white underwing mallard duck feathers attached to a string. The lower garland, at floor level, was composed of various plants, savory herbs, mints, and leaves.

The *Ku'ksū* dancer and escorts could now be heard walking around the outside perimeter of the dance house. The group did this four times, with bull-roarers in motion. Then the *Ku'ksū* dancer entered through the dancers' door as two singers stood in front of the drum and sang. The *moki*-clad performer did not actually dance, but rather ran and turned in sets of four. The dancer then laid a bundle of short dunning sticks before the village headman as a demand for payment.

"Let all pay," the headman said. "He has entered here and we will contribute beads and rope." Many went outside to their homes and brought in payments of shell, beads, cords, and other small valuables, which they laid down. Tokiwa laid down some shell beads.

The *moki* dressed *Ku'ksū* dancer was the most prestigious, most devout officer of the Secret Society and would appear on four successive days. The colors and elaborate feather ornamentations from head to foot exuded a divine essence.

Towards the end of the night's ceremony, the *moki* dancer and escorts stood in one line facing the spirit pole. A high shrill voice could be heard echoing from beneath the feather mantle. Was it the voice of *Aikat*, the people wondered? This vibrant singing voice warned:

"I am going to give you plenty of acorns. Those who have been lazy shall receive none.

"I am going to give you plenty of salmon. Those who have debts shall receive none.

"I am going to leave you plenty of spiritual power. Those who steal from others shall receive none."

The *Ku'ksū* dancer departed, returning down the same footpath and back into the same grove of trees from whence he had come.

Tokiwa watched as two other performers, both arrayed in feathers and paint, shinnied up the sacred spirit pole like trapeze acrobats and proceeded to hang by their legs from rafters, swaying their heads and arms, shaking clapstick rattles they held in both hands, while they sang. These two were joined below by a company of special dancers who shouted warnings and went looking for any bad spirits who might be inside the dance house.

The ridiculous *Peheipe* reemerged, performing for the amusement of the spectators. First the clown shouted to scare the men. Then he pretended to be afraid. He put on a coyote head over his forehead and carried two short sticks on which he leaned, stooping as if they were forelegs. He imitated the animal looking about, leaping upon an imaginary gopher and killing it, while another dancer described what he was doing. There was much laughter.

Afterwards Owa and Hoo-du-sa, the two silver-haired doctors, came forward. Each took a position at opposite sides of the massive spirit-pole which supported the roof. Resting their chins upon it, each doctor turned his face towards heaven, and, in turn, chanted short and solemn prayers to the spirits. Tokiwa joined in as the congregation responded, "Ho!" in approval. Often there were moments of profound silence, during which no one moved. Then everyone would resume dancing, while the drummer kept time by stamping on his foot drum.

In this manner the four days of ceremony—filled with a rich mixture of sacred dances alternated with episodes of comedy—passed quickly.

All of Tokiwa's fears about working with the Secret Society elders had disappeared. Owa and Hoo-du-sa had become like family, and through them he entrusted himself to the larger group. He stayed with the *yo-mi*, the curing doctors, and performed sacred rites with them for a total of thirty-two days.

Hoo-du-sa taught Tokiwa that the Creator had given the people three laws by which to live: love the Creator, respect wisdom, and help others. All three laws were symbolized in the people's creation story.

Hoo-du-sa advised Tokiwa: "The Creator should be loved like a father. He created first the earth, then the plants, then the animals, and finally humans; giving all of this to mankind.

"The World-Maker Spirit gave each man a woman to love and to each woman a man to love. This Great Spirit is in everything and told us, 'If you do as I tell you, then everything you do will be well.' "

Owa added, "Coyote disobeyed the Creator. He did not respect the Creator's wisdom, so Coyote's son became the first to die.

"Elders with wrinkled faces are like the gnarled trunks of our great valley oaks. They are the successful survivors who are on the good road, who know how to live. Listen to them when they speak."

Hoo-du-sa then continued, "Turtle said, 'All that has been done by the Creator is good.' Turtle followed the Creator's every instruction. Turtle dove to the bottom of the vast ocean to get good dry earth, which became our world. Turtle helped mankind.

"World-Maker created everything as beauty and so must every man create beauty in every thing he makes or does and in every path he takes.

"This same Creator helped mankind by giving us his sister, the sun, and his brother, the moon. The World-Maker also brought the people heavenly food, *ooti.* Through the giving of these gifts, we are shown how to act towards each other."

The doctors also taught about power and ways to make contact with the spirit world. Owa told these things to Tokiwa:

"When I dream, I am getting advice from one of the spirit helpers; sometimes it's Little Lizard, sometimes it's Cottontail talking. Sometimes it's my dead friend, Tokeeno. Dreams tell me how to live. They help direct my future.

"When I pray, I am talking to the spirit world. I am talking to the spirits in the sacred mountains shaped like sweathouses. Sometimes I pray to the spirits of the land you stand on. Sometimes I talk to the four winds. They, in turn, take my prayers to the Creator.

"When I pray, I speak whatever comes from the heart. I listen to the forces of the world. I am careful to sit still, in silence; to shut off my own internal talk and to use my ears to take some of the burden from my eyes. Then I hear the spirit-forces who live in the quartz rocks, in the sacred lakes, and on the moon.

"Training begins when one is very young. Tokiwa, use your senses of smell, look when there is apparently nothing to see, and listen when all is seemingly quiet. More powerful than words is silence with the people."

Now the doctors saw that the moon was fixed right by Coyote. The light of the evening cast a silver glow across the face of the southern-most butte—the one that most resembles a sweathouse, the one that has the *Ku'Kinim Kumi* spirit house inside. The spiritual power called *pe* is left over from the sacred time of creation, and is free-floating and obtainable.

In the morning, Owa, Hoo-du-sa, and the other doctors led Tokiwa to the mountain's ramparts and around to the "porch" on the west side where the sacred door was located. The entrance to the spirit house was still there along the steep terrace. Owa pointed to a great singular rock that lay on its side, weather-worn and covered with petroglyph markings left by the grandfathers.

"Tokiwa, see there is the entrance to the spirit house," exclaimed Owa.

Here, at this sacred spot, Tokiwa and the others prostrated themselves in prayer. Tokiwa began repeating over and over the words from his earlier dream. "Kick the rock three times and say 'Open'! " This incantation Tokiwa continued reciting throughout the night.

Dawn arrived and the group prayed again as the golden rays of morning sunlight broke through from the distant

"West Side of South Butte." Photo by Ted Rieger.

horizon. The pilgrims, who still fasted from any greases or meats, ate another frugal meal of unsalted acorn and bread.

Two days earlier, Owa had carefully dug sacred roots out of the ground along the river and gathered sacred herbs he took from Spirit Mountain. Only he knew about these plants which he planned to serve to Tokiwa. He believed that these plants contained spirits who could contact ghost spirits of the dead, especially supernatural guardians. Hopefully, in this way Tokiwa would contact Big Meadows.

After digging the roots out of the ground from under one side of each plant, so as not to injure or bruise the spirits, Owa washed and then cut them into four lengths and put them to soak in a large soapstone mortar. He then did the same with the special herbs. He asked the other doctors to bring the herbs to him two days later, along with serving baskets just before high-noon.

The time for giving Tokiwa the powerful medicines arrived. Once Owa was handed the medicines, he placed it into a new basket and handed Tokiwa a second basket, telling him to hold his basket with both hands in front of his chest. All the others now stayed downwind so their body scents would not blow towards the baskets. They said prayers to the four winds:

"Earth-Maker, the flaming God who has always been, help this man who is going to drink you. Help him gain knowledge from you, the powers of the world. Do not hurt this man who is going to drink you."

Tokiwa dipped with his basket containing the liquid and took a small drink. Soon he fell into a trance, becoming detached from any needs or concerns, yet remaining an extension of the larger group—linked to the invisible forces of creation. His vision now compressed time and space. He could see distant places and events. He could see into the future.

A voice told Tokiwa to run. He began running up the face of the mountain, all the while closely watched by the others.

Tokiwa saw a great eagle overhead, in the bright white glare of the sky. It was the same eagle which had been in his dream—the same eagle that had alighted near him and had taken him on his back to this very same mountain.

Tokiwa followed after the eagle for some distance. Though he had no body, as in a dream, his consciousness followed the flight of this eagle. They flew a long way.

"Where are you going?" the eagle asked.

"I seek spiritual power to use to bring health to my family and village," Tokiwa said.

"That is good," Eagle said. "You may have this. But you must also stay in good balance and learn of power from others around you."

"I seek also Big Meadows," Tokiwa continued, "I miss him and so does his family. I would like to see him and talk with him again."

"Big Meadows 'looked back,'" Eagle said. "He looked

back because he missed his loved ones so much. He is there among the deer, the very animals he himself once hunted. You do not want to talk to him. He is a ghost spirit! If you talk to him, you will die. Listen when he speaks to you. He will guide you."

Then Tokiwa watched the great bird descend to a lake, follow the bank of the lake and then alight on a log boat. Suddenly, Eagle disappeared. But there, at the center of the raft, was the form of the same ferryman he had met on his journey. Again, he sat with his back to Tokiwa, but this time he was wrapped in flaming feathered robes. Silently he sat, unmoving, his head thrust forward in deep thought.

That was all Tokiwa remembered.

When Tokiwa "returned" to the doctors, he was a wiser man. He had been fed "spirit food." The men around him agreed that his experiences were powerful and meaningful. He had also learned much from these Secret Society doctors; knowledge which he could now take back with him. He had learned that the spirit of Big Meadows would be his own life-long helping spirit.

The next day, Tokiwa rose, spoke with Owa and Hoo-du-sa once more bidding them good-bye, and then departed for home. A rain fell, then the sun shone and a beneficent double rainbow appeared, embracing the mountains like a halo, a blessing.

"*He iiiii!*" Tokiwa shouted in his exuberance.

He turned again homeward, wiser, with his heart full of happiness knowing he soon would hold Nesuya in his arms.

1801

The Acorn-Bread Season

7. Powerful Poisons

"When a doctor, you can never eat meat, salt, nor greases, otherwise you will die. Are you ready for this? Are you also prepared to have no marriage and do without women? You must sacrifice these things if you want to have power, as you will become so poisonous that you will kill anyone you touch."

Old-Grouse Woman, doctor

When Tokiwa returned home to *Yamanködö* from Spirit Mountain, foremost on his mind was marrying Nesuya and becoming a powerful doctor. But he held off from seeing Nesuya right away. Instead, Tokiwa saw his grandfather and family first, telling them everything that had happened during the many days he had been away. Woyectena, his mother, served up a big meal of barbecued salmon and tender greens. At So-se-yah-mah's suggestion, the grandson agreed to pay one string of beads for an audience with Old-Grouse Woman, the resourceful doctor in *Kadema*, and ask to be her understudy.

Tokiwa entered Old-Grouse Woman's lodge, gifting the string of beads. He remained cautious not to get in her shadow for this caused sickness. He noticed a bunch of feathers, some with black tips and some with white tips, suspended from a hair string. Were these not the special kind of feathers about which So-se-yah-mah spoke?

Once they began speaking, Tokiwa found another side to the doctor's personality. Aside from being respected and helpful, she was also suspicious of Tokiwa and very protective of her secrets. "Others try to harm me with their poisons," she whispered. "Have you heard anyone talking? I think it's those doctors in the hills. They're after me again."

"No, doctor," Tokiwa disagreed, "I have not heard any such rumors. I come to see you because I am interested in training under your tutelage to learn about powerful medicines."

"I don't like to talk about powerful plants with anybody," she returned curtly. "And why must you follow this thing to be a sucking doctor? Do you like learning to kill people?"

Old-Grouse Woman continued, "Training will be most difficult. It will take you two or three years before you can even be effective. As a doctor, you can never eat meat, salt, nor greases, otherwise you will die. Are you ready for this? Are you also prepared to have no marriage and do without women? You must sacrifice these things if you want to have power, for you will become so poisonous that you will kill anyone you touch."

Tokiwa felt the muscles contract in his throat. Then Old-Grouse Woman questioned him, "Is there a woman in your life? Is there one you plan to marry?"

A long silence came over Tokiwa. He could sense the lady doctor knew he was thinking of Nesuya. Old-Grouse Woman then walked over to the feathers and stared at them. What was she doing? Could she tell from the feathers? Yes, he had tender feelings toward Big Meadows' daughter. But he wouldn't tell Old-Grouse Woman this, not now anyway.

Tokiwa tried to change the subject. He spoke of his mystical experience at *Esto-Yamani*. She listened quietly as Tokiwa described as best he could the sacred roots and herbs which he had drank.

Old-Grouse Woman looked bored. "Nothing of what you learned could kill anybody," she concluded, "while my *ca'wen* can."

"Because I know your grandfather well and also because you think you are sincere about doctoring, I will tell you something about powerful poisons. This may help you to decide things.

"Many poisons occur in the air, the water, or the ground. There is one plant, if you smoke it, which can turn you into a bear allowing you to kill your enemies. Another kind grows over the ground like hair. Occasionally, I will show an old person how to put that medicine all over himself so he can turn into a grizzly. To change bears back into men, I select another medicine which must be smoked. Then the person has only to jump into the creek and he comes out a man again.

"Sometimes I use a very powerful medicine found in oak galls, or made from an insect's leg or white spider's leg. Then I blow the poison off my open palm like this, or 'shoot' the poison off on tiny arrows using a small bow made from an eagle quill with a woman's hair for the bow string. My *sila* arrows carry a poison which can work damage on enemies a great distance off. They fall or get knocked down completely."

Tokiwa was greatly impressed. He knew beforehand that Old-Grouse Woman was hired all the time to poison enemies or trouble-makers. His family knew a girl who refused her suitor after her family had accepted presents. This went against custom, so the suitor's family then paid Old-Grouse Woman to kill that girl, which she did. Old-Grouse Woman explained, "One way is to put one seed from a small plant called *halky* into the victim's mush. A second way is to follow the victim until he or she urinates. Then I put a stick treated with special medicine into the wet spot. I say, 'This person shall die at such and such a time.' Parents," she continued, "are very afraid that their children might die this way so they tell them to make water over a bush so as to scatter their urine and protect themselves."

Tokiwa sensed the lady doctor could go on forever about her knowledge. But now she became silent for a long time. Tokiwa sat confused. He truly admired the craft and wisdom of doctoring, but he also wanted a life with Nesuya.

Frustrated, Tokiwa asked, "But what of my dream-vision that tells me to be a *yo-mi* like you?" he asked. "What about the eagle who told me that I must stay balanced and learn of power from others around me? Doesn't this mean that I must learn from you?"

Old-Grouse Woman would not answer. "You ask too many questions and you listen too little."

She proceeded to take out her *dokdok*, doctor bag, which was filled with powerful substances. Frightened, Tokiwa moved away, covering his eyes and nose with his hands, for he knew that the sight alone of the insides of this bag could make one's nose bleed.

"Don't worry," the doctor laughed, "I'm not going to show the insides of my bag to you. Look away for now if you wish."

Tokiwa obeyed, relieved that nothing happened.

Finally, he was told to turn around. He found the doctor lying down and lighting the sacred pipe, using a pitch stick she lifted slowly from the fire. The pipe was two feet long, made of manzanita, with a soapstone bowl at the end. Normally, women did not smoke, but she was no normal woman. First, she puffed repeatedly and inhaled to get the pipe started, as sacred tobacco smoke wafted upwards, becoming caught in the draft from the round smokehole above, and continuing up on the road to Heavenly Valley.

There was silence again.

Then Old-Grouse Woman inhaled slowly, swallowing the smoke. Soon her head fell upon her breast with her eyes closed. But she was not asleep. After another long silence, she spoke. Tokiwa would never forget her words. "Very soon the next destruction will come. 'Bad spirits' will run through the Valley People like a fire through grass, and a great many will be gone.

"The people will need the greatest strength imaginable. They will need 'spirit food' from the doctor.

"Right now, you are not an exceptional person. You have good in your heart and will become poisonous only when the time is right. But never become a spirit doctor while you have women in your life, or you might kill them.

"I tell you this to let you know; to tell you to listen to your spirit helpers by doing what sets well in your heart."

This finished, Tokiwa paid Old-Grouse Woman a second string of beads. Now he knew: he had to put aside his quest to become a powerful doctor. He didn't want to learn how to kill anyone. There were no warring enemies. There was no sickness. The most important thing now was Nesuya, and he would have her.

1801

The Ashy Season

8. A New Family is Born

"There were good reasons for restraining a baby instead of allowing the infant to crawl and explore the world on its own. A tied-in baby rarely fussed or cried. Also, it caused the baby to 'watch' and 'receive' the world instead of being raised to set out and conquer it. Self-centered independence was curtailed."

It had been almost two months since Tokiwa had seen Nesuya. He went to *Kadema*, but she wasn't there. The people told him she had moved with her mother to *Pusuni*. They said Wypooke had elected to marry her late husband's brother, Matos, the powerful hunting captain there.

Tokiwa right away took this as bad news, for Ya-hai-lum also lived in *Pusuni*, and Matos and Ya-hai-lum were allies.

Matos was a very large man physically, six feet three inches. Like his brother, Matos had many bearskins and was a high ranking *Yĕ'poni* as well. Because of his great success as a hunter, the people afforded Matos many chiefly privileges. For example, he was allowed more than one wife. Indeed, Matos had two wives and Wypooke became his third.

Wypooke moved to *Pusuni* without any real choice, for

women never lived alone. Of all her late husband's brothers, Matos was her best choice. He could provide the most security and protection for herself and her daughter. But immediately upon arriving Wypooke found that she had her hands full. She was the third wife, and the newest one did the most work.

"The younger two only cook the meat," Wypooke complained to everyone. "I gather wood, pound acorns, prepare the mush, clean house, mend clothes, and don't have time to make my baskets."

Now the battle was on. All three women bickered and ridiculed each other. The quarreling went on through the night. Finally, Matos had had enough. He grabbed up his bear hides, some gear, and made them think he was about to leave for good. He was really going fishing.

"Don't be like that or I will leave you!" Matos yelled. "Then you will be sorry! You grumble all the time. Nobody is going to stay married to you. You are already old women. Don't be like that. Behave instead and feed your man well!"

They soon quit quarreling.

Matos decided to take one of the wives along to the mountains. The next day he would take another wife to the mountains. Finally, he would take Wypooke, the newest. Only when he followed that order, did they keep peace. If he declined to take one of them with him, she grumbled. He would be served a poor breakfast and a poor supper greeted his return.

Only chiefs and special hunters had two or more wives, usually sisters. An important chief usually had three wives and slept between two while he put his feet on the third one who slept crosswise at the foot.

Tokiwa arrived at Matos' lodge when the big captain was away. But Nesuya and the wives were there, as well as Ya-hai-lum and a number of older men who were strangers to Tokiwa.

"Nesuya, who are all these old men who camp at your door?" Tokiwa wanted to know. "Are they friends who hunt with Matos?"

"No, they are suitors wanting me," Nesuya answered nervously. "My new father has told me to choose from one of them in spite of the fact they are all twenty years older. They are all good hunters and brave fighters. My father says they all have wealth."

"But at *Kadema* we already have shown the people we are not lazy," Tokiwa argued. "I brought good meat to your lodge many times, and you brought my family acorn meal. Does Matos know this? Does your new father know that I was 'tested with arrows' in initiation and that I am a brave man?"

In response to all he said, Nesuya gave Tokiwa a big hug, while all the other suitors watched. "My heart wants you and no one else," Nesuya whispered. "I want us to grow old together. I will tell my family so."

The next day, Tokiwa returned and found Matos with Ya-hai-lum laughing and talking together. When Tokiwa approached them, Ya-hai-lum got up and walked away.

Their plan is perfectly clear, Tokiwa thought. It's so obvious, why didn't I recognize it before? Together they schemed the murder of Big Meadows to get him out of the way so they both would benefit! Matos becomes the "big hunter" of the entire region and is accorded more chiefly privileges. This even puts him in line to possibly become chief. And Wypooke, the widow, has to move in with Matos as his third wife. Nesuya, of course, must move as well. Hence, the remainder of Big Meadows' wealth gets transferred to Matos. Ya-hai-lum, on the other hand, for his involvement in the murder, gets Matos' approval to marry Nesuya... But to step forward and say all this requires proof, proof that I don't have, Tokiwa realized.

Finally, Tokiwa got an audience with Matos.

"I am Tokiwa from *Yamanködö* who loves Nesuya. I am one who wishes to marry her. I have no wealth right now, but I am willing to hunt and get bearskins, many bearskins, for shell-bead money. I have known Big Meadows and Wypooke for many seasons and they speak highly of me. I will be a good man for you once I gain your approval to marry this girl."

Matos responded, "You speak well of yourself Tokiwa."

Suddenly, Wypooke was standing with her back to Tokiwa and addressing Matos. She pretended she didn't see Tokiwa.

"Good husband, you have met this fine young initiate, Tokiwa, whom I told you of before. He is never lazy and is the best suitor for our Nesuya. His youth will keep our larder full with deer meat in those years when we grow old. Tokiwa is young, but he has the power of the *Yẽ'poni* to protect our family. Because you are known for your wisdom in matters of importance, you will recognize that young man will be a good husband for Nesuya."

No more was said. Thereafter, affairs improved for Tokiwa. By the month's end, Matos told Ya-hai-lum and the other suitors to stop their visits. There was no other choice. Matos feared Wypooke might turn the other two wives against him. Ya-hai-lum, though angry, had to go find some other wife.

Tokiwa's family recognized that Nesuya's family made him the final choice. They gave a "Big Time Without Dancing," which was like an engagement party.

Now, cautiously and according to custom, Tokiwa moved into the bride's household. He was expected to help support Matos, the father-in-law. The mother-in-law and son-in-law taboos became fully enforced. Tokiwa would no longer look directly at Wypooke nor the other wives. They all pulled deerskins over their faces whenever Tokiwa approached. Neither could he look into the face of Matos or his brothers.

At first, Tokiwa and Nesuya were instructed to sleep away from each other on opposite sides of the fire-hearth. If Nesuya had stayed up all night or resisted Tokiwa's advances, he would know he wasn't welcome after all. For several days, her parents told the couple to sleep apart. Then, each night, Tokiwa was permitted to sleep closer to Nesuya.

One night the parents announced, "Let them sleep together. Let the man put his bed within touching distance." That night they consummated the marriage.

Nine months to that night, the couple's first child was born, a big baby girl whom they named Nopanny. With the arrival of children and adequate wealth, the couple moved into their own house. They returned to *Yamanködö* to build their home among Tokiwa's people. All of this the couple accomplished in their first year. It was a happy time.

Nesuya kept baby Nopanny tightly swaddled in a baby basket made of willow rods lashed on a forked branch. This forked branch enabled Nesuya to stick the cradle with baby into the ground vertically, freeing her to complete other chores.

There were good reasons for restraining a baby instead of allowing the infant to crawl and explore the world on its own. Maidu-Nisenan villages were always next to rushing water. Other dangers were grizzly bears, rattlesnakes, scorpions, poisonous plants, and neighbors who kidnapped babies. A tied-in baby rarely fussed or cried. Also, it caused the baby to "watch" and "receive" the world instead of being raised to set out and conquer it. Self-centered independence was curtailed. The restrictions of movement during these months greatly influenced Maidu-Nisenan temperament and personality.

When Nopanny was first tied into her cradle, the grandmothers installed a "rock pillar" set for the purpose of flattening the back of her head. In one week's time this was achieved—a mark of beauty in the eyes of the culture.

The grandmothers also helped to provide baby diaper material by collecting cat tails. Nesuya would pack this absorbent material in the baby's cradle basket. She was watchful, replacing it as necessary. Like other Nisenan mothers, Nesuya was always particular to keep things clean.

Of all his grandchildren, Matos came to love Nopanny the most. She was such a happy baby. He would make special visits to see her. When he returned from trips, he always brought her presents—perhaps a small feathered "treasure" basket with abalone shell jewelry. Sometimes he brought her soft fox skins.

1806

The Falling-Leaf Season

9. The Coyote Spirit

"Coyote died that time
But he came back.
He always does.
That fellow cannot be killed
for long."

Coyote Man

While Nopany was just a little girl, she earned her name which literally meant "Little-Sharp-Ears." It was the Maidu-Nisenan custom that children were not to be given their names until the people had first determined the child's heart. Then the proper name could be given.

In this case, the family chose "Little-Sharp-Ears" because in the mornings, when the little girl would first awaken, she would hear the coyotes howling in the woods. With big dark eyes, she would ask her parents, "Who is it that howls to me in the woods?"

Tokiwa would say, "It is Coyote, the evil one. He wants you to listen to him and do what he says instead of watching and listening and doing what your family wants of you. He is the trickster while we are your parents. He reminds us that there exists both Good and Evil in this world. The coyote spirit, who changes the moon for us, is good. The coyote force, who devours his own dead, is evil."

"If Coyote is evil, why hasn't anyone killed him?" Nopanny asked.

Tokiwa and Nesuya thought for some time and then Nesuya responded, "People did try once. People were angry with Coyote. They all agreed that everyone should come in from north and east, from south and west, and crowd all the coyotes into the center of the country, and then they would kill them. But there was one ridiculous Coyote who was the *Yĕ'-ponim* with dominion over all of man. He was one of the primordial elements of the world. Protected by sacred powers, he cannot be killed for long. He is a survivor. He always comes back.

"Look at Coyote with his two yellow eyes, with his gaunt, tawny body and gray belly. Look at him always slinking and skulking around the outskirts of our village, hunting gophers, scavenging the refuse pile, and even stealing salmon and deer meat from our drying racks! Many animals, like the elk and bear and wolf, cannot tolerate too many people. But Coyote can. In spite of traps and poisons, coyotes live—and they always will. Beware, they may even inherit the world someday!

"In time, when the people realized all this, they gave up trying to kill Coyote. So, whenever he cries, he is telling us,

"Coyote, setting the moon," photo by John S. Jackson.

'Coyote can never be killed off.' He laughingly says, 'I am Coyote, and can never die. People may kill me, but there will always be coyotes left.' "

"Father, have you ever killed a coyote with the bow?" Little-Sharp-Ears asked.

"No," Tokiwa answered. "Why would I ever try? None of us will ever kill any coyotes because a coyote may also be somebody's relative. When people die, they go to the big assembly-house to the north, the roundhouse of the dead. There is a bridge, and if the dead slip and fall in, they become a fish. And when a man or woman who has many children dies, and they look back when going, they turn into a coyote or deer so that they can see their loved ones from time to time. They look back on purpose so that they can meet with them once in a while, when they walk in the brush. So we do not shoot a coyote even though we have a bow, and we shoot only some deer."

Nesuya held her daughter's face up close to her own. "My little one," she said, "always in this world Good and Evil will oppose one another. Good is in our songs, our dances, and seen in the stages of the moon. Coyote is of the air, and of the fog. The rainbow is made of Coyote's urine."

That night "Little-Sharp-Ears" was permitted to sit with the old people inside the dance house. Normally little ones were not allowed inside because they became frightened. But that night there were more stories about Coyote and everyone thought "Little-Sharp-Ears" should hear them. The old people told her that in the ancient times the Creator spoke these words:

"Good is the wisdom of life which I have now awakened from the earth. Evil is nothing more than the ignorance of this life. In life, there ever dwells both Good and Evil. Always, in the world, these two elements will oppose one another.

"Good must resist the pull of the invisible Evil,

for if Evil should ever become all-powerful, then soon again there would be nothing, as it was the first few days of its creation. Life would quickly vanish.

"Coyote looks like Evil should, knows what Evil is doing and always does it first; tries to awaken Good to that which is Evil. In no other way will Good, which never sees true Evil, ever know where Evil is or how Evil works.

"Coyote likes the games he plays, ever loud and full of humor, ever full of tricks and cunning. And Good, seeing Evil in Coyote's antics, must flee in mortal fear of his games.

"No matter what Coyote does or says, always do the opposite... only then can life continue. Only then will this tree we sit beneath forever stand, giving nourishment to the greatest life yet to come. From now on, this is what you must do.

"This is the way you must do 'till the world shall be made over."*

Nopanny learned these words which the Creator spoke during the earliest days of the world's creation. In this manner she was reminded that whenever anyone tattles or does dishonorable things, they are compared to Coyote.

Walking to their home that evening, Tokiwa carried the tired Nopanny and continued to speak of Coyote, "To this day, the people wing their arrows with three feathers because Coyote's arrows always have just two.

"Coyote is many things, Nopanny. He is the greedy, gluttonous fool for all the people to see. Yet, he is also the god-spirit and benefactor because he teaches the people the

---

* Adapted from Richard Simpson's book *Ooti: A Maidu Legacy* by written permission of the author and of the publisher, Celestial Arts in Berkeley, California.

way through his mistakes and failures. Nevertheless, little one, he is also clever enough to rebound and find another way, never giving up. Coyote is the trickster. He would have many women, young unthinking girls and even the wives of other men. He is an evil schemer who is meddlesome and a spoiler of plans. Nopanny, never forget, this is the role of the Coyote force. This is who he is, and why he never really dies."

"Coyote # 1" by Nisenan artist Harry Fonseca.

1806

The Acorn-Bread Season

10. Ḱ-öi (War)

"That Chucumne is a brave fellow," Matos said, carefully aiming his arrow. His shot carried low, skimming close to the surface of the ground all the way.

There were over five hundred autonomous tribelets in California—little nations really, most of them numbering no more than a few thousand people. Each group tended to live along a river, more or less set apart from neighbors. Each group believed that its territory was the center of the world; that they were the more civilized people and that it was the "others" across the river who did things wrong. It was "they" who were quarrelsome, treacherous, and the aggressors.

Ownership of each of these territories, rested in the community or political group rather than the individual. Within the boundaries of the community the individual could hunt, camp, fish, and gather food anywhere. But when one little world ventured outside its own territory and into that of another's without permission, and with the intent to take food supplies, then this was trespassing, an act tantamount to war.

War was chiefly over food supplies because the valley was rich in resources, while the hills were poor. Sometimes the hill people would poach in the valley. Transgressors would sometimes strip an entire oak grove of its acorns. Sometimes a quail fence would be emptied, or fish would be taken from another's fishing station. Feuding also resulted from raids for brides, from retaliation for acts of revenge, and from doctors "poisoning" people.

The Nisenan-*Chucumnes* grudge was a long-standing one. As far back as could be remembered, the neighboring *Chucumnes* were the Nisenan's bitter enemy. Long ago, the Nisenan say, they controlled both sides of their river, the *No'to-mom.* The *Chucumnes,* with their different tongue, lived along the Cosumnes River drainage to the south. But gradually, the *Chucumnes* started moving northward. In recent years they had successfully taken over most of the south bank of the *No'to-mom.* Now it appeared that the *Chucumnes* wanted even more Nisenan territory. It got so bad that they would kill a Nisenan for the slightest provocation or for no reason at all. They were trouble. It was better to stay on one's own side of the river so no one would get killed. But soon there would be more killings. When things got really bad, the chiefs would call a war.

One day Humpai, one of the two headmen at *Pusuni,* announced that his family was being poisoned one by one by a *Chucumnes* doctor who lived south across the river.

"We were poisoned," Humpai told the others. "Ooey-muck-ney, my mother, died after pounding acorns and making acorn soup. Soo-soot-ney, my uncle's wife died the next day. And now Hawl-lie, my elder brother, the one who was to be made chief, died yesterday."

The others agreed that Humpai must be correct, so they helped him pay Old-Grouse Woman to kill this evil *Chucumnes* doctor. Old-Grouse Woman prepared *sila,* the poisoned sticks.

"Before I shoot them off," she said, "you must take me across the river by boat and with guards because the victim lives far to the south."

The doctor was escorted across the river where she shot them off. The days passed, and although the *Chucumnes* doctor hadn't died yet, the people were confident that he soon would.

Humpai's payment, to kill the doctor in revenge, might have left things resolved. However, some *Tahn'-kum* men had come to a stream (which in modern times came to be known as Oregon Creek) and captured one *Chucumnes* woman and two men, all of whom had permission to trade. For an unknown reason, they killed the men and tied the woman to a tree and burned off her hands and feet. The victim somehow crawled part way home before a *Chucumnes* search party found her. Before she died, she revealed that her assailants were Nisenan. For this, people were certain the *Chucumnes* would soon seek revenge.

When Tokiwa heard about the woman being tortured, he thought of the story of the two *Chucumnes* warriors who killed his father. Since it was never precisely determined which *Chucumnes* warriors had killed his father, his people arbitrarily captured two *Chucumnes* men and held them prisoners-of-war. In the winter, his people performed a ritual torture known as the "shooting" ceremony. The dancers tied one captive to the center pole of the dance house where they ceremonially executed him. Woyectena, Tokiwa's mother, was allowed to shoot the captive. She said she shot several arrows into each captive which inflicted pain without doing mortal injury. Other forms of torture accompanied this "shooting" ceremony. Big Meadows finally put an end to each victim's suffering by spearing them.

Now came more news. A runner entered *Yamanködö* and all listened.

"The message comes from headman Tawec in *Kadema*. Some *Kadema* women were attacked by *Chucumnes* yesterday. Two of the women hid. They were on their way downstream to our grove of marked trees when our women saw six *Chucumnes* men wading across the *No'to-mom.* They hid and observed these men whipping down acorns out of our trees. The men then chased after our women, trying to kill them with knives. That is the way those *Chucumnes* men are. But our women ran fast and escaped.

"When I, Tawec, heard of this, I hurried to the grove," the runner continued, "But they were gone. They have taken many acorns. Had I been there and not the women, I would have killed those *Chucumnes* there under the trees myself."

Runners carried this news to the other twenty-five closely allied Nisenan villages from *Pusuni* at the mouth to *Wa-pum-ni* under Chief Tucollie to the east. Headmen from many of the villages gathered to decide what to do.

Tawec, however, demanded payment first. He sent another runner to toss twenty dunning sticks into the lodge of the *Chucumnes'* headman. Each stick had a ring painted around the end, representing demands for payments. While it was a reproach to any Indian to have dunning sticks thrown into his lodge, it was a bigger insult if the person was a great chief. But the *Chucumnes* leader refused to acknowledge the debt notice. He merely ignored Tawec.

"Shall we send a raiding party at dawn and surprise those *Chucumnes*?" several people then asked. "We can kill everyone except the good-looking women. These we can carry off and include them in our households or sell them to some distant tribe."

Some liked this plan. Others thought it too severe. They feared survivors would only retaliate and carry off their own women later.

"But something has to be done," they said. "That *Chucumnes* doctor poisoned our chief's family. Those men raided *ooti* from our trees and chased after our women.

Now their chief will not honor our chief's demand for payments. Who do those *Chucumnes* think they are?"

So all the headmen went into council. Many watched the sky and felt the air. Something had reached into their inner beings that said now was a proper time to call for Ḱ-öi. The war signal, the Coyote cry, could be heard clear across camp. By relay, the cry was passed on to all the other camps, in short order.

The community council sent a brave man to carry a bundle of seven arrows to the *Chucumnes* chief. The number of arrows indicated the number of days to elapse before the armed confrontation. Both sides now saw they had seven days to make ready.

With the declaration of war, both sides of the river swarmed with activity. Warriors constructed or mended their armor made from elk hide, which covered their bodies from the knees to the shoulders. Others made armor from straight round sticks of mountain mahogany or serviceberry wood, bound into a waistcoat with cord twining. Waistcoat armor, with a high collar, enabled the warrior to withdraw his head entirely from an approaching wave of arrows.

Other warriors tested bows, lances, and slings, making certain that only arrows with eagle feathers were used.

The headmen went round discussing the strengths and possible weaknesses of each warrior. They announced who would be their war captain and who would be their "brave man," their special champion, called a *hudessi*. The *hudessi* must be fast and agile, dodging anything he saw coming at him.

Matos went off with Tokiwa to get poison for their arrows. It was now the hot season, so they went into the rocks to find rattlesnakes. Big, strong Matos, who was more afraid of snakes, followed after Tokiwa, who jumped gingerly from rock to rock. Tokiwa tied deer liver onto a stick and carried it with them.

"Quick, move away!" Matos yelled, as Tokiwa turned around and found the first rattlesnake almost underneath his bare feet.

The snake's triangular head darted this way and that. Tokiwa kept pricking it with a long stick, making it angry. When it was angry enough, he pointed the liver at the snake and the snake bit it. The liver turned jet black. Only then did Tokiwa allow the rattlesnake to go. Neither of them would kill the rattlesnakes they found, for it would be bad luck. Now they smeared their arrows with the liver and let them dry.

As they returned to camp with the poison, Tokiwa spoke confidently about the pending war, "Now we have the poison. Their men will not dare get near us. We will hold our ground."

But Matos looked down. "There is something about this war I don't like. I will be happy only when this war is over."

The appointed morning finally arrived. The ceremony of war began with its ritual and regularity. The two armies walked, each with sixty to seventy warriors, to the traditional battlefield, a ridge used in earlier wars. This spot was upstream from *Kadema* on the south side of the river on a level shoulder of hillslope. This spot was originally chosen because of the many small round stones in the adjacent dry river bed, ideal for slings.

Matos was the designated war captain for the Nisenan army. He gave out the hideous war signal of the Valley People, Coyote's cry, "*He iiiii!* Slender and shifty Ya-hai-lum was announced as the Nisenan's *hudessi* or "brave man" killer. He would have to move this way and that, dodging all the arrows.

Saving of face was most important. The war would not be settled if one of these "brave men" were shot. Peace could be made only when neither "brave man" was

wounded; when neither army ran and there was a
stalemate. If after several exchanges of shots, no one was
hit, one headman could then propose cessation of
hostilities, saying, "Each side proved bravery. We are
sufficiently satisfied. Now we can be friends."

Moreover, whenever there were killings, the side who
killed the most would have to pay for the dead on both
sides. The "victor" would have to pay the highest price,
thus discouraging warfare altogether.

The chiefs of both armies watched from a higher knoll
upstream. The armies took up their positions just one bow
shot apart. Both lines stood with their sides to the enemy
and kept in constant motion, like their *hudessi*, to make a
poor target. The warriors had painted their breasts black.
The *Chucumnes* looked especially ominous this time
because they had also waxed and twisted out the fore-hair
on their heads to look like two horns. These were topped
with feathers.

Using a stick, the chiefs drew a line on the ground
between the two camps. Then from both sides one arrow
was shot. The camp whose arrow hit farthest from the line
would have to put up the first man. The *Chucumnes* shot
their arrow first. There! . . . it landed. Matos then carefully
released his arrow. There! But it did not land as close.

So Ya-hai-lum stood out in front and the enemy took a
volley at him. This brave man killer moved this way and
that, dodging all the arrows. The arrows whizzed by him:
There! . . . There! . . . between his legs . . . everywhere he
moved to dodge those arrows. When an arrow came very,
very close, he moved slightly and the shaft always missed,
the feathers grazing his body. He stayed safe this way all
afternoon. Back and forth the arrows flew. The warriors
tried not to advance nor retreat unless someone was hit.
Each warrior dodged and exchanged shots on the spot.

After each discharge of arrows, the children, by mutual

consent, were sent into the ranks of the enemy to pick up the poisoned arrows which had missed their mark. Each child returned the arrows to the quivers of their parent, only to be sent again running into the enemy's ranks.

At first, the women of the villages protested against the war. As a result, the war was almost stalled off. But not showing up for the prescribed day of battle, which they themselves announced, would have resulted in a severe loss of face. Payments would be demanded.

Still, the men could not restrain their wives' protests. At last big Matos stepped into the heated dispute. He shouted back at all the defiant women, "Stop! Stop this talk! We must show all enemies around us that our Big Chief has warriors and that we are not a bluff. Otherwise, those same enemies will someday make slaves of all of us."

Reluctantly, Nesuya and the others went back to pounding acorn meal.

The men waged war for several hours. Meanwhile, the chiefs continued watching the fighting from the knoll. Chiefs Tawec, Humpai, Teduwa, and Tucollie now sent out messengers with orders that all married women must begin dancing for power, while their men fought. Women usually allowed one day, maybe two, to pass, then they danced through the night. But Nesuya and the other wives started dancing early this time to transfer extra power and good luck to their men.

Matos, the war captain, reached into his quiver and drew out a poisoned arrow. All day long he had watched the enemy's brave man dodging arrows.

"That *Chucumne* is a brave fellow," Matos said, carefully aiming his arrow. His shot carried low, skimming close to the surface of the ground all the way. Somehow the *hudessi* did not see the approaching arrow. Instead, he stood still and, suddenly—the arrow pierced him in the breast to a depth of nine inches. Backwards he fell to a sitting position, spitting up blood.

The other *Chucumnes* warriors gathered around their wounded *hudessi*. Half-frozen in disbelief, they were a pitiful sight. Upon seeing Matos and his army charging after them, they ran. Pursued by spears and slings, three more *Chucumnes* warriors were then killed.

When Matos reached the badly wounded *hudessi*, he knew the poison would soon kill him. The dying man was still conscious. He looked up at Matos—the man who had shot him—and warned, "If you kill someone, sooner or later you pay for your meanness. Somebody will take your favorite kin and you will grieve the rest of your life."

Immediately, Matos thought of Nopanny, his favorite granddaughter. "No harm must come to her!"

Some of the *Chucumnes* returned and had heard their *hudessi's* words. Then they ran off again because they saw the Nisenan club bearers coming.

The club bearers were the "finish-up" fellows. When a man was shot, the club bearers said *"Tuj, tuy!* Don't waste arrows, leave him!" Quickly they went behind the wounded *hudessi* and shouted, lifted up their clubs and killed him.

The Nisenan "victors" then made a dummy resembling the brave man they had killed and shot it full of arrows, using enemy arrows they picked up from the battle area. The defeated army, by custom, was expected to come and bury their own arrows and swallow the shame of seeing the dummy representing their brave man shot full of arrows. The real body itself was also shot full with arrows collected from the enemy's battlefield.

The *Chucumnes* refused to return to bury their arrows. Therefore, the Nisenan named them cowards. "There can be no peace or friendship now," Chief Tawec muttered.

The Nisenan warriors now headed home except for Matos and three others who had killed someone during battle. They were required to fast all the way home and all night. The next day they went down to the river to swim and clean themselves. Only then could they come back and eat.

Days passed. *Peheipe* So-me-lah wrapped himself in bearskin and posted himself atop the dance house each night to guard against any surprise attacks. The men took shifts sleeping, always keeping guards posted. Matos worried about blood revenge.

Months went by. For a time, the people tried to forget about their foes. The clown finally relaxed his watch.

Sometime later, Matos, Tokiwa, and some of the others left on a hunting trip. While they were gone, a *Chucumnes* raiding party crossed the river and attacked at dawn. No one would ever discover the treachery of Ya-hai-lum who, through the meanness of his spirit, told the *Chucumnes* about Nopanny and the way to Tokiwa's lodge. They clubbed Nesuya and left her for dead, carrying little Nopanny off with them.

When the hunters returned from their trip and heard the awful news, they broke down and wept. They organized a search party—searching for weeks. But Nopanny was never found.

Tokiwa and Nesuya eventually recovered, for ten years later they would have a second baby girl who would help sooth their pain. But for the rest of his life, Matos grieved for his beloved granddaughter, Nopanny.

1808

The Falling-Leaf Season

11. The Arrival of Whites

"I got down from my horse and found that she was in fact dead. Could it be possible, thought I, that we who called ourselves Christians were such frightful objects as to scare poor savages to death?!"

Jedediah S. Smith

Little things always precede great changes. Swarms of new honey bees, never seen before, joined the bumble-bees in pollenating the flowers in Maidu country. Occasionally, cattle, hogs, or the amazing horses were discovered living in the meadows or foothills. Subtly, the balance of things was changing.

One day, in the Falling-Leaf Season, Nisenan runners ran ahead with news for all their villages and the *Koni* Plains Miwok villages. From the west, they brought exciting news.

"Something has come down from the sky. Strangers without family, who speak an unfamiliar tongue, have come from the western edge of the world, the ocean," they said. "They are on their way to this country, to your villages, to your side."

Headman Tawec ordered that both a night watch and a day watch be kept. Tokiwa, Matos, and the other men took turns.

More runners came into camp. "The newcomers from the sky are built like all of us, only some have blue eyes and light hair. All of them have blood that is very light, for none of us are as white in skin-color as they are."

"Are they god-like?" the people asked. "Are they super-natural beings like *Ku'ksŭ*, the first man, and Morning-Star Woman, the first woman, who both were also very white? Do they have special power like the white goose, the white deer, and *O'-lele*, the white luck bird?" Some thought this was so; that the strangers were god-like; that they were very white because they were creatures who made it to heaven and back and that's why they were white.

Time passed. Again the report was that others had seen the light-skinned beings. This time they were camped along the Cosumnes River. The light-skins were encroaching steadily closer. Reports left the people uncertain and confused about what these newcomers wished.

Matos, the war captain, asked, "Why do they have no wives nor children with them? They all are single. Without family, they are troublesome and less important than these bugs crossing the trail. If they were not aiming at some mischief, then why did they not stay at home among their own people?"

Old-Grouse Women, the doctor, stepped forward into the discussion. "There are other things about the strangers I don't like. They know of 'poisoned sticks' like we doctors," she said. "Only their poison comes out of long solid sticks which shoot little round things a long distance. They have something short that shoots just the same."

This news scared the people.

Two days went by. For a time, the people tried to forget these reports. They were so awful to think about. But the day all the doctors foretold approached. From the south, came the very light beings. Immediately, the people became frightened. The creatures neared the village.

The headmen and doctors disagreed upon the action to be taken. One chief said, "Let us do this. We must go high into the mountains and wait."

Just as quickly another headman stood up and said, "No, let us do this. I have a better idea to protect the people. There is a doctor from the north, named Curly Headed Doctor, who has taken a long cord and painted it red. He placed it around his whole camp. He has said that the strangers will fall down and die if they touch the string; they will never be able to cross it. This is what we should do here," the headman said.

So now it was that the people's headmen and doctors began quarreling among themselves about the best way to handle the problem. People panicked, and everybody began shouting at each other, fighting one another.

All of this came about when Ensign Gabriel Moraga, the tall, well-built, fairly dark complexioned man of forty-one years, left on the 25th of September 1808, from Mission San Jose. He led the first non-Indian expedition to penetrate Maidu and Nisenan territories. Moraga, by superior order of the Governor of the Province of California, Don Josef Joaquin de Arrillaga, was accompanied by one corporal and eleven privates on a reconnaissance of the rivers to the north to see if some good spots could be found for new missions. Moraga had the reputation as the best California soldier of his day. He was to look for Indian *rancherias* or villages, as well as capture any *cimarones*, runaway Indians. According to the theory of missionization, the native came to the mission voluntarily. But once there, he or she was bound to remain.

Moraga and his soldiers went mounted on horses, taking remounts with them. Each wore leather chaps and a low, shortbrimmed hat. Their armaments consisted of a gun, a cartridge pouch, and a great lance. They carried an *adarga*, an oval-shaped leather shield made of two thicknesses of cowhide. Also, for protection, they wore their *cueros* made of five thicknesses of animal skins and of sufficient thickness that the arrows of the Indians could not harm them.

Moraga and his men spent the first night safely in Livermore Valley, after having traveled about six leagues (one league equals about 2.75 miles) to the north. After ten more days of traveling, they camped, on October 5th, on the Cosumnes River, less than half a day's journey south of Nisenan territory. This was when the Indian runners had headed north and east to bring the news and when the in-fighting among the Indians had started.

Gariel Moraga recorded these events into his diary:

6th day of October: "Today I sent four men upstream up the Cosumnes to explore it to the place where it leaves the Sierra. They found good plains, pine timber and many Indians.

"I went north-northwest with two men, and after about five leagues, I found a river which runs from north to south. It carries more water than any of the others except the San Joaquin.

"This is all today."

7th day of October: "Today we broke camp on the Cosumnes River and continued in the same direction to the river discovered yesterday (American River), to which we gave the name *Las Llagas* (River of Sorrows) to commemorate the sufferings of Christ in being crowned with thorns.

"This afternoon I went upstream with two men, and in about 4 leagues we found the Sierra [explored present Folsom-Auburn areas] but I did not enter because it was very late."

By October 8th, the Indian elders were in such disagreements that almost everyone fled for the time being, crossing to the west bank of the *Káyimceu* (Feather River). Women and children were escorted still farther north to villages along the Bear River. The warriors regrouped and waited anxiously, placing themselves between the white invaders and their sacred mountain. Tokiwa, Matos, and Ya-hai-lum, now united against a common enemy, protested angrily as Moraga's soldiers crossed the *No'to-mom* (Las Llagas) near *Kadema* and continued to penetrate Nisenan territory for the first time and without permission.

Matos, still the war captain, complained bitterly to everyone about the trespassing that violated Nisenan law. "Long ago this valley was staked off," Matos began. "The land has never belonged to just anyone. Different elders own and have marked certain big trees under which these strangers now camp. Others own certain meadows through which the strangers now transgress."

Tokiwa now stood to talk. "The strangers have seized some of our lands and now are heading for Spirit Mountain. They will desecrate our sacred places if they aren't stopped. The *tankus* (the people) must fight them here on the *Káyimceu.*"

The men around Tokiwa shouted approval. Together they turned towards Chief Tawec and awaited his response.

Tawec spoke. "This is the very last river the light ones need to cross to move right up towards our sacred places. Here we must stop them."

On October 9th, the strangers moved up to the *Káyimceu.* When three of them crossed at a place where they could successfully wade, Tawec ordered Matos and the warriors to charge them. Matos and Ya-hai-lum attacked carrying spears, while Tokiwa advanced with his bow drawn back. Matos threw his spear and hit one of the strangers in the face. Blood poured from his nose.

But Tokiwa discovered that his arrows could not penetrate inside the soldiers' armor. Well placed arrows, again and again, deflected down to the ground.

Ya-hai-lum ran right up to the strangers, but fell lifeless, killed by one of the stranger's long solid sticks.

Seeing this and the other strangers advancing with their long sticks from the other bank, the rest of the Native defense broke ranks and jumped into the river to swim away. When this day had ended, Gabriel Moraga recorded this account into his diary:

9th day of October: "Today we broke camp and moved to the river discovered yesterday, which we named the Sacramento [Feather River]. They have measured this river at 169 *varas* [one *vara* equals 33 inches] across and uniformly from one shore to the other a *vara* and a half deep.

"There are many Indians on this river, and they showed themselves completely hostile, for this afternoon I sent three men to ford the river, and having found a ford, they crossed. On seeing them the Indians on the other bank took up arms against them. They lightly wounded one soldier, cutting one of his nostrils by a sharp object which they threw at him on a stick like a lance, which they use with flint blade. The result of the matter was that one Indian was killed, and the rest jumped into the river and swam across... This is all there is to note today."

After this first battle, the people pulled back farther under the protection of their sacred mountain, *Esto-Yamani.* Everyone was terrified of the strangers' powerful "poisons" and apparent invincibility. On the next day when the light ones crossed the *Káyimceu* and marched farther north, headman Tawec decided instead that the people must try to talk and receive payments from the strangers for the harms they had done. So one day later, on the 11th of October, one hundred and thirty Konkow Maidu and Nisenan warriors escorted Tawec and the brother chiefs, Humpai and Teduwa of *Pusuni,* to try to talk with the strangers. Teduwa, who knew parts of many languages, was able to work with a mission Indian interpreter the strangers had brought along with them. Through him, the chiefs spoke to the strangers asking what they wished.

The warriors formed a long line with weapons drawn, as the three headmen walked slowly to a place in front of the strangers. Moraga, the leader, beckoned all to come closer. But since all were within hearing distance, Tawec stopped where he was and spoke first.

"You have trespassed across our lands. This land does not belong to just anyone. You have killed one of our people. We wonder who you are and why you are here?

"Who is your Creator? Do you follow the cross sticks religion taught at the missions or do you listen to the great voice of Nature? Or are you our enemies?"

After a short discussion, the interpreter responded, "We are followers of the Christ whom we remember by the crossed sticks. We will not harm anyone. But we are enemies of those who wish to be our enemies. If you wish to be friends, we will be your friends."

Again, Tawec put forward the question, "Will you harm us?"

"No," the translator responded.

Hearing this, Tawec then turned around to look at Tokiwa, Matos and the other warriors. "Put down your weapons and come sit up with us," Tawec waved.

Immediately, the Indian warriors loosened their bows and gradually approached, even to the point of seating themselves at the place where the strangers were all mounted on horseback. Tokiwa and Matos wanted to see the horses more closely. They even wanted to trade for some. Motioning for the strangers to dismount, Tokiwa and Matos persuaded five of the strangers to do so.

"Have my fine hunting bow," Tokiwa offered. "We give you weapons for your horses." But the light ones' leader did not permit such payment. The weapons were handed right back. Instead, the strangers only permitted

Tokiwa, Matos and the others to touch and look at the horses, and the conversation came to an end.

Traveling now along the Big North Water River, the strangers rode eight leagues farther northwest and then turned back returning along the same route from which they had come. On October 13th, Moraga and his men spent the night safely on the *Rio de las Llagas*, discovered on the 6th.

14th day of October: "Today we followed the same route. I sent the corporal downstream with four men, and he sighted many Indians along its banks [American River]. He couldn't reach its mouth because of the abundance of tules.

"We arrived at the river discovered on the fourth [Cosumnes River], called San Francisco, where we spent the night safely."

23rd day of October: "Today we arrived at Mission San Jose, concluding the expedition without any other trouble than is noted on the ninth day of the present month." *Gabriel Moraga*

For twenty winters (1808—1828), the Maidu and Nisenan rarely ever saw more of the light strangers, who came from the edge of the world without family. An occasional hairy-faced, mountain man, who came to trap and trade for beaver skins, would pass through. But they were no trouble.

Life, however, was never quite the same. The Maidu and Nisenan continued to hear from the west how the strangers were making other Indians build more missions for them. Runners told how some of the mission Indians said the padres were kind, but that every soldier was cruel and dangerous. Some of the Indians would try to run away only to be caught and whipped by the soldiers.

The people learned how the white leaders always went

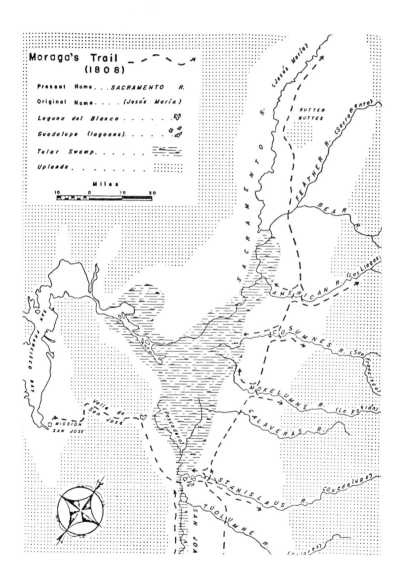

Moraga's Trail.

around with crossed sticks, wore the long brown robes, and poured sacred water onto the people's heads. They kept telling the people they were lost souls; that the Great Spirit is a human being who lives up above the clouds somewhere. They said there was a son of this Great Spirit who came to live on earth. He died in a very bad way to save the people and that was why they must worship him. Those who resisted the strangers' religion were beaten.

One day Tawec, the headman at *Kadema,* spoke out against this white man's religion, saying:

"Those ideas are strange. To us the Good Spirit is in the sacred lakes and mountains, and in the sky everywhere. With a wide sweep of his arm, the Creator caused every star to shine. We have the moon, which is the Creator's brother. And we have the sun, which is His sister.

"In the end it will not make much difference what mission there is on the outside. We have always had the Good Spirit within our hearts. This is the heart which counts. This is the heart which will remain long after all the outside missions have rotted away."

One major event for Tokiwa and Nesuya was the birth of another daughter, who they named Yototowi. Yototowi came from the Good Spirit some ten winters after they had lost Nopanny to kidnappers. Tokiwa was very pleased. He doted over this second baby much like big Matos had doted over their Nopanny.

Ten more winters passed on, and pretty Yototowi was almost eleven when the Jedediah Smith party arrived.

1828, The Big Moon Season

Jedediah Smith and his party of mountain men were the first Americans to come to California by the overland route and the second non-Indian expedition to intrude into Maidu Indian territory.

Jedediah Smith had little in common with other moun-

tain men, who admired his courage and leadership. Smith
was soft spoken, very literate, and a very devout Methodist
with high standards. He would not winter with different
Indian women each year as the other men commonly did.
He was a tall American, and 29 years old at the time he
entered Southern Maidu country in 1828. He had an
extremely handsome face and went clean shaven, unlike
the other mountain men who sported heavy beards. Having
barely survived an attack from a great grizzly five years
before, an awful scar was kept half hidden to one side of his
face, covered by hair and sideburns. The grizzly had nearly
torn off one of Smith's ears. But, fortunately, another
trapper had successfully sewn the ear back on with needle
and thread.

All through January, February, and March, Smith's
party of twenty trapped beaver up the streams that rushed
into the Sacramento River from the east—the Cosumnes,
the American, the Bear, and the Feather. In St. Louis, the
beaver fur sold for $5 a pelt, which was ultimately pressed
into felt material to make the tall dress hats that were in
fashion for men at the time.

The expedition had horses and pack mules. They also
carried powerful Hawkins rifles to kill game for food, to
prevent Indians from getting near their steel traps, and to
fight off troublesome grizzly bears which they encountered
a number of times.

In the "Big Moon" mid-winter month, Jedediah Smith
recorded these "wild" events along the American River
involving the Nisenan Indians he came upon.

20th of February: "Two Indians Killed.

"A considerable body of oak timber along its
banks, Indians by hundreds but wilder than
antelopes running and screaming in every direction.
It appeared to me that the farther I traveled north
the Indians became more numerous.

"The river [American] on which I encamped I called Wild River. I determined to change my course and make a trail towards passing the mountain. I supposed that the snow had become sufficiently hard by that time to bear my horses. I therefore turned east and at first traveled up Wild River and then took the divide between Wild and Indian Rivers. For the first two days I found no snow, the traveling not worse than might be expected. The timber thus far principally oak and on the second day some very large cedar.

"Indians were numerous and I was frequently passing their little villages of 10 or 12 little circular lodges made of old trees and bark. During these two days the Indians collected in great numbers around me at two different times. I endeavored to convince them of my disposition to be friendly by every means in my power but to no purpose. They considered all my friendly signs caused by my own weakness. Of our guns they had never seen the effects and supposed them solid sticks which we could use in close contest. Whatever may have been their views they pressed so closely and in such numbers on my party that I was obliged to look for an advantageous piece of ground on which to make a stand against the threatened danger.

"Having found a favorable position I again tried to convince them of my friendly disposition but to no purpose. Their preparations were still going forward and their parties were occupying favorable points around me. Seeing what must be the inevitable consequence I determined to anticipate them in the commencement and wishing to them as little harm as possible and yet consistant with my own safety I ordered 2 men to fire (of course not the most uncertain marksmen). I preferred long shots that it might give them the idea that we could kill at any distance.

"At the report of the guns, both men firing at once, two Indians fell. For a moment the Indians stood still and silent as if a thunder bolt had fallen among them, then a few words passed from party to party and in a moment they ran like deer.

"The other afray was similar to the above described except that more guns were fired and more Indians were killed."

26th of February: "Another Indian Killed, One wounded.

"I went hunting and killed a goose and an antelope. Two of my trappers, [Toussaint] Maréchal and [John] Turner were up 3 or 4 miles from camp and seeing some Indians around their traps who would not come to them but attempted to run off they fired at them and Turner killed one and Maréchal wounded another.

"I was extremely sorry for the occurrence and reprimanded them severely for their impolite conduct. To prevent the recurrence of such an act the only remedy in my power was to forbid them the privilege of setting traps, for I could not always have the trappers under my eyes.

"*27th;* fine weather but still so muddy that I was afraid to try the country north. I went down the river a few miles, in doing which I fell in with an Indian who could not handily get away and coaxed him to camp. I made him a few presents and sent him off."

"*1st of March:* "10 Year Old Indian Girl Scared to Death.

"I went in company with the trappers down to

the confluence of Wild River [American River] and
the Buenaventura [Sacramento River] which was
about 2 miles from camp. The Buenaventura still
continued about 300 yards wide and came from the
north maintaining the appearance of which I have
before spoken. The mountains on each side were
about 30 miles distant."

O   O   O

Tragically, it was on this same day that Tokiwa was
trying to escort his wife, daughter, and mother back home
to *Yamanködö*. All of them had come from visiting Matos
and Wypooke in *Pusuni*. While there, runners came into
the village and told about the recent killings of Indians by
white strangers who lurked close by. As a precaution,
Tokiwa had everyone stay over in *Pusuni* for four days
before attempting to return home. Since there was no more
bad news, and hoping the trail would now be safe, they
departed.

Half way to *Kadema*, they stopped off momentarily to
rest and visit friends at *Sek*, a smaller village. While they
were inside a lodge, suddenly people could be heard yelling
and screaming outside.

"The strangers are coming this way, so run!" warned
the *Peheipe* from the roof. "Be careful how you step. Don't
get killed."

Panic ensued nonetheless, as the light strangers
swooped down upon the people. They came galloping on
mounts, down the very footpath on which the people fled.
Tokiwa grabbed hold of Nesuya and Yototowi, his daughter,
and led them towards the river. Tokiwa yelled to his
mother, "Quick, everyone to the water!"

The three jumped down the bank to the river's edge.
Nesuya and then Tokiwa stepped into a log boat they
found. Unbeknown to the parents, Yototowi was no longer
with them. She chose not to board the boat. Perhaps she

knew there was not enough room for all four on the boat. Perhaps she was more worried about her grandmother, Woyectena, still behind. Instead, the ten year old turned around and tried to run away down the footpath in the opposite direction.

Unfortunately, she ran right into some of the strangers. They were uglier than she had thought them to be. They all had hairy faces like a bear's, save for one who was clean shaven. She noticed that this one had spotted her. Every stranger carried one of those dreaded solid sticks that shot the deadly poison she had heard about.

Yototowi now spied poor Grandma Woyectena. She had been overtaken and made captive by one of the hairy-faced strangers. Would they kill her? Yototowi started towards her. But when the grandmother spied her granddaughter, she screamed, "Run, run away, Yototowi!"

For some distance, Yototowi continued to run away fast, her body flushed with fright. Her heart beat so fast until she stumbled over, falling to the ground, dead.

Jedediah Smith completed his diary for that day, 1st of March 1828:

"In going down Wild River we came suddenly on an Indian lodge. Its inhabitants immediately fled. Some plunged into the river and some took a raft while some squaws ran down the bank of the stream. We galloped after them and overtook one who appeared very much frightened and pacified her in the usual manner by making her some presents.

"I then went on to the place I had seen one fall down. She was still laying there and apparently lifeless. She was 10 or 11 years old. I got down from my horse and found that she was in fact dead. Could it be possible, thought I, that we who called ourselves Christians were such frightful objects as to scare poor savages to death!?

"But I had little time for meditation for it was necessary that I should provide for the wants of my party and endeavor to extricate myself from the embarrassing situation in which I was placed. I therefore, to convince the friends of the poor girl of my regret for what had been done, covered her body with a blanket and left some trifles near by, and in commemoration of the singular wildness of those Indians and the novel occurrence that made it appear so forcibly, I named the river on which it happened 'Wild River.' To this river I had before that time applied a different name."

As soon as Tokiwa and Nesuya discovered that they had left two members of their family behind, Tokiwa struggled frantically with the boat's paddle-blade to make their craft return to the same bank they had left. The strong current delayed their return. First, they found the grandmother unharmed and with presents, though still shaken. Next they found their daughter, Yototowi. Her still body lay along the footpath, covered with a red woolen blanket with some presents. The grief-stricken parents and grandmother fell down to their knees by this river's edge in the deepest of sorrows.

1833

The Big One Season

12. River of Sorrows

"One day the people saw a bad omen. A coyote suddenly appeared in the Valley, in the hot, middle part of the day— something coyotes never do."

For the next five years following the Indian killings, and after Jedediah Smith's party had left the *No'to-mom* for good, life ripened into golden times for all the Maidu and Nisenan peoples in the Great Central Valley. The Creator blessed the trees with plentiful harvests of acorn and buckeye. The hunts for deer and elk were always successful. So rarely did any of the people get attacked by bear or bitten by rattlesnake that they seemed to forget that, in life, both Good and Evil dwell.

While there were gains, there were losses. Both So-se-yah-mah, the grandfather and dance captain, and Old-Grouse Woman, the poisonous doctor, had departed to Heavenly Valley. Tokiwa had kept their memories. At night, Tokiwa, who had become a venerated story teller himself, told the village children some of the funny and sometimes perverse stories of Coyote, and how Mouse stole fire from the Thunder Being;* stories that So-se-yah-mah had told Tokiwa when he was growing up. Tokiwa would also tell the fascinated children about Old-Grouse Woman;

* Refer to Appendices C, D and E.

about her séances, poisonings, magic, and how she would always whisper so low.

Tokiwa witnessed still more changes in Maidu and Nisenan life. Chiefs, for example, were being selected differently. Now, it was *who* you knew rather than *what* you knew and *what* you had. Those who spoke Spanish had direct access to the trading goods from whites, thereby language usurped the traditional qualifications for becoming a chief.

More horses appeared. In the ravines and canyons, the people captured these runaways from the ranchos and missions to the west. The people never rode them. Instead, they traded these creatures to the "big chiefs" who traveled down the trail from Oregon and Walla Walla to the north.

Beautiful glass beads could be had from the Canadians based at Fort Vancouver (Hudson's Bay Company), who wanted beaver pelts in trade. The Maidu-Nisenan hunters would give four or five pelts for either one string of beautiful beads, a red wool scarf, or for one handkerchief.

"Slave trading" was also big. Indian raiding parties came from everywhere, looking for young boys and girls to kidnap. Rancheros and Mexican soldiers, who came through, sometimes looked for young slaves too. Many of these captured Indians would run away. Whenever a mission runaway or *cimarone* came to the Maidu or Nisenan camps seeking refuge, he or she was readily taken in. When the soldiers asked, "Are you hiding any *cimarones!*" the Nisenan answered, "We don't know."

During the "hot" season in the fifth year (1833) since the Jedediah Smith party had left, the invisible Evil came in the wind, singing Old-Grouse Woman's prophecy told to Tokiwa many years before; that "bad spirits" are in the world and that before long a great many Indians will die.

One day Tokiwa saw a bad omen. A coyote suddenly appeared in the valley, in the hot, middle part of the day—

something coyotes never do. The creature stopped, stared, and then trotted away over the horizon. It was the sign for the destruction of the people. Good could no longer resist. The fur trappers brought the invisible Evil to the valley: malaria.

This deadly visitor became all powerful, with death most severe along the rivers in the Valley, where the mosquito injected the single cell parasite into the bloodstream. Upon entering the body, the tiny parasite became lodged in the liver and multiplied. Fully 40,000 people of the Great Central Valley died in 1833.

The people suffered chills and fevers from the malaria. The fevers were attended by fits or convulsions and shaking at regular intervals. Deaths escalated so quickly that many never received proper burials. The survivors soon abandoned their villages and fled in despair only to die along the sloughs or streams elsewhere.

The pestilence came in a fury like wind across water. In some families, all of the children died within the same week. Fathers, mothers, grandparents all died, the plague having no mercy for any particular gender, age group, or position.

When a mother died suddenly, leaving a very young infant, the relatives, by custom, had the duty to destroy it. There were no milk cows whatsoever, no bottle-nurturing. A grandmother or aunt would hold the baby in her arms, and while it sought the maternal fountain, pressed it to her breast until it was smothered.

Day and night, at every village for several weeks, came the incessant, most terrible wailing sounds, heard all across the valley. The living covered their faces with pine pitch, over which they threw ashes so that they were not recognizable. At first, the dead were bound for burial with ropes, their knees brought up to the chest. But many were placed into shallow graves, while most never got buried at all, as the terrible scourge magnified. Piles of fresh human bones were tragic sights everywhere, remnants left over by carrion eaters. Dwellings became void, villages desolate.

The survivors wailed bitterly. Some stood in silent grief around certain graves. Still others would cross their hands over their heads, pressing down as if to relieve the pain of sorrow, all the while making a piercing cry as if the heart could not stand its grief.

Tokiwa became sick, but somehow survived; but not before suffering the death of Nesuya, his beloved wife. Alone, Tokiwa painted a black streak horizontally across his face between his nose and chin. Whenever the streak "ran" from his crying, he received comfort. Relatives and friends came to grieve. They burned beads and property to seal their friendship with him. The death of Nesuya affected Tokiwa greatly.

When the Evil force first came to the *No'to-mom* villages, the Secret Society *Yĕ'poni* elders gathered together to talk. They noticed the deaths happening to all the Valley people, while all of the Hill people remained unscathed. One elder spoke out.

"The deaths we are suffering are because of the killings of Opuley and Ho'mah men in the *Pitchiku* dance house."

"Ho!" another *Yĕ'poni* agreed. "The Hill people are the only ones who live. The runners have seen it. It must be true."

"Look how they hurl *sila* sticks from long distances," added a third *Yĕ'poni*. "When they lost their relatives, they got mad. They got very mad. Those Hill doctors sent bad air into the Valley to avenge those killings. I believe they are talking to this poison air," he continued, "They're telling it, 'Go to such and such places and kill everyone.' They're telling it to groan like a sick man."

Then the *Yĕ'poni* elders and the doctors decided what everyone still alive must do to get rid of the bad poison air.

The headman gave decisive directions, "First, each of you are to clean your house. Both sick and well must do this. Place all ashes, filth and spittle you collect in old baskets for which you have no further use. Then set these baskets of refuse out front of your houses. It will be picked up and carried away."

It took three days and the people were dying. Then the headman gave more instructions, "Now you must follow me and the other *Yĕ'poni* to the river. We will march in a certain order. The women and young boys must pick up and carry the baskets. They shall join the march as the procession passes. By then we will have 'caught' the thing that is causing the sickness and we are going to drown it.

"Let the oldest *Yĕ'poni* march first with the doctors. Then the young men and boys shall follow behind me, after that the old women, and lastly those carrying the baskets.

"You sick people do not have to go on the march. Others can go in your place. If anyone has a sick child, one may stay with it and send a replacement."

Now the procession started for the river. The *Yĕ'poni* painted their faces and arms and looked as powerful as they could, all in black and red. They wore angelica, wormwood, and baywood leaves in bands or as brush around their hips. The doctors shot their little arrows made for the purpose of shooting the pains away. The men carried whistles which they blew. But otherwise they made no sound. Then the women followed, groaning.

But even after the people had discarded their baskets into the river, many people still died. So other cures were tried. Every house hung their *yo-kóli* or flag made of a willow pole with strings of white feathers tied at one end. The white feathers, when hung atop the people's lodge, was said to ward off sickness.

Also, the women proceeded to plaster acorn dough "marks," set in designs, to the outside of the bark door to their lodges to prevent bad luck. If the marks were not made, they said, all sorts of ill luck would happen, such as falls from the pine nut trees and snake bites.

Yet, all of these rites came to no avail. They saw family members, who weren't sick before, starting to get sick and die.

"Evil is here because we have not lived well," some of the people now cried. "We didn't give enough at the last burning. We didn't wash ourselves and atone ourselves at the last World Renewal Ceremony.

"The Creator is angry with us because the Secret Society failed to follow the Creator's instructions in keeping the sacred rites," others stated.

Now the destruction of the people became nearly complete. The people were without runners. There was no more news coming in. They were lost. Everyone was sick and dying. Tawec, their chief, died also. Now the people were without their great headman to give them proper advice. Their world was almost over, having no headman and no spirit doctor to give them hope, power, and strength.

Those very few who survived tried to take up a new life. But it was never like the old ways. Up to ninety percent of the local population, numbering in the thousands, were decimated. Families, friends, and the well-knit village structures were gone.

In the aftermath of the destruction would come John A. Sutter. The Gold Rush would follow just nine years after his arrival. It would bring stampeding hordes of European-Americans traveling through the Maidu and Valley Nisenan homelands to reach Sacramento and the gold fields. Then it would become the Hill Nisenan's and Mountain Maidu's turn to meet their destruction. Miners would stake their claims on the Indian's territory, would cut his oak trees for fuel, would hunt his game for food, would trample his bulbous roots in digging for gold, and would invade his family by taking young Indian women, willing or not, for servants and wives. The gold seekers also would bring in other diseases, namely, smallpox, tuberculosis, cholera, and venereal diseases to which the Indians had no resistance. The dense populations and extensive village organizations of the Maidu-Nisenan cultures, which had existed in the Valley and the hills for centuries, were almost gone. The Indians were so decimated that they could offer but a shadow of opposition to the gold-mining flood which swept over them in 1849. Once there were 8,000 to 10,000. By 1910, the Maidu and Nisenan—including those of mixed bloods—had declined to 1,100.

1839

The "Big One" Season

13. The Indians' Story of Sutter

*"In the first boat, the Walagumnes Indians saw a white man,
wearing a straw hat, dark vest, and white cotton pantaloons.
In the days to come, he would be known as "Tscheba" or
"Chief" by the Feather River Indians; and called Don Agosto
by his Spanish-speaking friends."*

As the scourge eliminated the people in the Great
Valley, John Sutter came in from the edge of the world with
ten *Kanakas*, natives of Hawaii, and a pet bulldog. The ten
were eight men and two women (the wives of two of the
men), who came to help develop the Valley for food. They
came in boats up the Big North Water River and *No'to-mom*
and set up Sutter's house across from *Pusuni*. Then Sutter
recruited enemy *Chucumnes* to work for him.

After the "dying" began, it happened that a lot of the
surviving Nisenan, especially people from *Pusuni*, congre-
gated at *Kadema*. Headman Tawec of *Kadema* had died. His
replacement was a likeable man named "Mike" Grimšo (in
Spanish; later written as Cleanso) who was born and raised
in *Pusuni* and married Dolores, a Konkow Maidu woman.

Tokiwa, however, moved up into the sacred Buttes to be close to the feather rope and his family spirits. He was in his 58th summer when Sutter arrived.

For Tokiwa, the signs had been clear. He was now fulfilling the role of a curing doctor. With the tragedies that befell his own family and bad spirits which still killed the Valley people, his destiny came from the law of the Creator that causes all things to be balanced in the end; the law that says all wrongs must be righted, that all things must be paid for. Tokiwa studied with both curing doctors and religious doctors who lived between *Kadema* and Sacred Mountain. This time he became quite poisonous. Tokiwa became more and more convinced that all of the non-Indian elements were responsible for the demise of his family and other Maidu-Nisenan kin. He knew it was only through vision quests and prayer that the old ways would return.

Chief Anashe of the *Walagumnes* (probably Miwok), whose major village was some twelve miles south from the mouth of the *No'to-mom*, was the first Indian leader to usher Sutter into the territory. In the late summer of 1839, Chief Anashe received daily reports of white men with "Indian" slaves and guns who were slowly traveling up the Big North Water River in three boats, making their way toward his camp. Hiding in trees along the river banks, hundreds of eyes now watched these boats, while, just up river, spirit doctors hurriedly tied strings of white mallard duck feathers to tree branches that overhung the river. The spirit doctors reminded the people that the white feathers were protective feathers of the Creator with the power to ward off evil.

Runners announced that the boats were almost in sight of Chief Anashe's village, so the chief continued with his war plans. He and his warriors dressed for battle. They painted their bodies red, black, and yellow. The warriors began a dance to prepare for war. They sang, clapped, shouted, and ululated shrilly. The strangers would either stop and pay for trespass privileges or be killed.

The sounds grew louder and louder. This clamor quickly penetrated the woodlands and carried up and down the river. It startled the hearts of Sutter and his loyal crew of *Kanakas* on board the pinnace, the lead boat. The hostile sounds scared the crews of the schooners *Isabel* and *Nicolas* so that they stopped their ships dead still in the water. They lowered their sails and dropped anchor. These crews, who were behind Sutter, were more afraid for themselves than for their own captain's safety.

The first encounter inside foreign territory, little explored beforehand, became indelibly fixed in Sutter's mind. Chief Anashe's group was surprised to see copper-colored people "like themselves" on board this first boat. It's likely that a special leniency was given the Sutter party because of them.

But who was this man Sutter?

In the first boat, the *Walagumnes* Indians saw one white man, wearing a straw hat, dark vest, and white cotton pantaloons. In the days to come, he would be known as *Tscheba* or "Chief" by the Indians along the *Káyimceu*, and Don Agosto by his Spanish-speaking friends. By the end of ten years (1839-1849), Indians who were closest to Sutter remembered him in one regard as a generous and outgoing man; as a romantic colonizer after fame and fortune. Yet, on the negative side, Sutter was "slaving Indians," was always drinking, and was quite a womanizer. He was also a con man who would take from Peter to give to Paul. Sutter was all these things. More than any other one white person, he would most affect the land-use of their territory and the course of their lives.

Whether it was for survival or because Sutter didn't like to lose face, or simply as a shrewd ploy in hope of gaining favors, Sutter did what most people would *not* do if they were in his situation. Sutter ordered his Hawaiian crew to row him ashore, directly into this dangerous-looking throng of aborigines who were armed with bows and arrows, slings, spear throwers, and clubs. Sutter told his loyal crew to carefully make firearms ready, but to hold their fire unless he expressly directed them to do otherwise. Alone and unarmed, Sutter jumped ashore.

Gambling on the likelihood that there were runaway mission Indians amongst the group, Sutter quickly called out in garbled Spanish, *"Adios, amigos! Adios, amigos!"*

There was nothing—no response.

Then two Indians pushed their way through the crowd. They spoke Spanish! Chief Anashe had sent forward two of his men who spoke the white man's tongue. They talked with Sutter in pidgin Spanish.

One of the Indian interpreters asked of Sutter, "Why do you come, strangers? Do you come in war?"

"I come in peace," Sutter returned quickly. "I have no Spaniards with me. I have not come to make war or to carry off your women for slaves," Sutter emphasized. "I have come only to live among you as a friend."

Sutter then produced some of his trade goods. He told the two interpreters to tell their people that he carried many more presents which he would distribute just as soon as he located his future home. A treaty of sorts was quickly drawn up whereby Sutter promised, "If you will come to me when I have landed, your presents will be given you."

With this first deal secured, Sutter felt better since he had some kind of legal agreement to show others. Brilliantly, Sutter chose not to break this initial contact with the Indians lest the "savages" change their minds. He promptly put the two Indian interpreters to work helping him. One he sent off in a tule boat with a letter for the crews of the *Isabel* and *Nicholas* who invariably were still "in hiding" down river. Sutter took the other Indian aboard the pinnace and made him pilot and interpreter.

Chief Anashe's *Walagumnes* were satisfied with the treaty and rushed off to neighboring villages to pass on the news about the gifts. Indians continued to watch Sutter wherever he went. Everyone watched for him to finally land, for they were after the goods.

Once Sutter had landed and established camp, he posed as a friend by giving the Indians beads, blankets, and shirts. He kept his earlier promise by also giving the Native people brightly-colored handkerchiefs, bags of Hawaiian sugar, red calico cloth, and steel fish hooks. Through this gift-giving, some of the Indian people from the south were induced to stay on.

Sutter showed these Indian people his power by making a terrifying noise, nine times, with his "brass thunder tubes," (cannons) as the boats *Isabel* and *Nicholas* were leaving back down river. This noise was dreadful and deafening and astonished all who heard it for the first time. A large number of deer, elk, and birds were startled. Howls of coyotes filled the air.

Sutter continued to play one group against another in order to take control of a large part of the Valley. With a home base established, Sutter now needed, most of all, to create a reliable food supply both to sustain the members of his colony and to have something to trade to build wealth. Sutter's choice was wheat.

To get labor, Sutter gathered together the chiefs of the whole area. Mike Cleanso worked for Sutter, but not at first. Chupuhu and Renufio were two more headmen who worked for Sutter. Also, there was Maximo's people from the *Mokelko* villages (*Chucumnes* or Miwok) who lived along the *Mokelumne* River. He took all of them to his home base christened *Nueva Helvecia* (New Switzerland) where he called them captains. As captains, the village chiefs gathered together Indian workers and took them to

Sutter's camp. First, Sutter directed the Indian men to hunt for him and to trap beaver, then to construct a large building of sun-dried adobe bricks; while the two *Kanaka* women taught the Indian girls how to wash and sew. Mud and straw were mixed together and kneaded by the Indians stomping in it. Then, it was carried to other Indians who poured the mixture into large moulds to form brick-shaped squares. Lastly, the squares were dried in the sun.

After an Indian had worked for six months, he was presented a necklace pendant made of a round of tin stamped with a star and six holes. A star with three holes signified three months' work. This was a special accounting system so that the Indians would not be bullied or cheated out of their pay by the white men. The people traded their tin disks at Sutter's store for whatever goods they wanted. Sutter refused to accept these disks from anyone but an Indian, preventing other white men from cheating the Indian people.

These things did happen, but the big testing time for Sutter was throughout the troublesome year of 1840. For instance, the Maidu-Nisenan, who had not learned about horses through Spanish mission contact, soon discovered that horse meat tasted good. Sutter had to stop several from killing his horses for food and to stop others from wounding his cattle as well.

In 1840, several proud *Chucumne* leaders to the south began plotting Sutter's murder. They came to resent how their own power was being usurped by this outsider. They became distraught as they saw more of their members doing Sutter's bidding. So one night after midnight, two *Chucumne* warriors with knives were sent in quietly through the dark. Their mission was to kill Sutter and then seize the settlement. Both approached Sutter as he chatted in French with Octavio Custot, a clerk.

The first Indian uttered a deep-throated cry, *"Heiii!"* (This to the Indians was to forewarn the soul of the victim.) Sutter just froze at first; then as he attempted to escape, his pet bulldog catapulted forward and gripped the Indian's throat in its vice-like jaws.

"O, Senor!" the Indian screamed, and everyone came running over to the scene and found the *Chucumne* held prisoner in the jaws of the bulldog. No sooner had they dragged the first Indian into the light when there came another scream. That same bulldog had trapped the other man.

Captain Sutter questioned the two sternly. Because they confessed and because Sutter needed to keep a work-force at the time, he did not kill these men. Rather, he took silk thread, sewed up their wounds, spoke again to them sternly, and then let them go.

This is how Sutter's bulldog saved his life, and why the two men went away free.

Sutter then got word that just to the south, two to three hundred *Chucumnes* were massing to attack. About these events, Sutter wrote:

"In the spring of 1840, the Indians began to be troublesome all around me, killing and wounding cattle, stealing horses, and threatening to attack us en masse. I was obliged to make campaigns against them and punish them severely. A little later about 200 or 300 was approaching and got united on Cosumne River, but I was not waiting for them. Left a small Garrison at home, cannons and other arms loaded, and left with 6 brave men and 2 Baquero's in the night, and took them by surprise at daylight. The fighting was a little hard, but after having lost about 30 men, they was willing to make a treaty with me, and after this lesson they behaved very well, and became my best friends and soldiers."

Sutter, about this time, then went to the Nisenan villages at *Pusuni* across the *No'to-mom*, as well as up river. These Nisenan had been afraid of their enemies, the *Chucumnes*, already working for Sutter. But Sutter gave more presents and arranged a kind of peace treaty between the tribes. So then Captain Mike Cleanso and other Nisenan headmen brought workers who also began working for Sutter, alongside many *Chucumnes!*

Pioneer Heinrich Lienhard, who lived at the fort, told how this ". . . Bushumne tribe [really *Pusuni* Nisenan across the American River from the fort] . . . subsequently proved to be his [Sutter's] most capable workers."

The Nisenan started to help build the fort then. Later Foothill Nisenan and *Chucumne* labor, together, began the building of a second flour mill on the upper Cosumnes River.

Soon Sutter was employing the Nisenan and *Chucumnes* in many new ways. Sutter and the *Kanakas* taught the Indian peoples to dig deep ditches around the fields, to irrigate the gardens, and work the land. Indians also had jobs as millers, bakers, cooks, gardeners, wool spinners and weavers. Others served as drivers and vaqueros and even sailors. If the Indian workers stopped to rest, the Indian captains were coerced into punishing their own people with cowhide whips. Several of these Indian captains completely sided with Sutter. Some locked up other Indians in rooms or penned them up in corrals so they could not run away at night.

To get meals over in a hurry so that the Indian workers could accomplish more for Sutter, the Indians were served all at the same time. They were fed a thin porridge of boiled beef mixed with wheat, in narrow troughs of hollow tree trunks like stock animals. Non-Indian guests ate separate from the Indians, and were served beefsteaks, eggs, beans, coarse bread, and tea.

Forty Indians served as bodyguard soldiers for Sutter. They were shown how to fire muskets. Fifteen mounted Indian soldiers wore green jackets with red cuffs, while twenty-five infantry wore blue jackets with red cuffs. For a time, Sutter took great pride in personally drilling his Indian soldiers. These Indians with guns worked for Sutter!

What convinced the local Nisenan and others to stay with Sutter was a retalitory raid Sutter successfully launched against the San Jose chieftain Acacio, and his cruel *Chucumne* warriors. With a mission pass granted them to visit "relatives," the *Chucumne's* engaged in murder and wife-stealing at the *rancheria* of *Yalesumne* along the Cosumnes, while the *Yalesumne* men were away working for Sutter in the fields. A sole witness, an old man, had dropped out of sight when the raid began by jumping into the Cosumnes River and crawling into a beaver's hole where he stayed. Afterwards he went north and told Sutter.

Sutter's answer was action, leading twenty white men plus a host of Indians in pursuit. They overtook the raiders about thirty miles to the west, just as the captives were being dragged on board rafts in the river. Sutter's party succeeded in freeing the captive girls. Seven of the abductors were killed outright and some fourteen Indian kidnappers were taken prisoner and herded back to *Nueva Helvecia.* Sutter told all the local Indians to assemble on the third day, allowing time for the word to spread. The captives were then summarily executed by a firing squad. This first mass execution *everyone* remembered, and it convinced the local tribes that Sutter would aid them against Indian attackers.

But while Sutter got the Indians on his side by putting down Indian kidnapping, ironically John A. Sutter himself was often involved in the dirty business of Indian slavery. He wrote to Antonio Suñol on June 1842, for example, promising to deliver some "little Indians." He made a practice of "adopting" the children of Indians killed in his punitive campaigns. These children were then distributed to friends as servants to earn Sutter goodwill, extension of credit, forgiveness for unpaid debts, and so forth. Sutter wrote to San Francisco merchant William Leidesdorff:

"I will send two Indian girls, of which you will take which you like the best. The other is for Mr. Ridley, whom I promised one longer than two years ago. As this shall never be considered as an article of trade, I make you a present with this girl."

When Sutter delivered another Indian girl to the wife of a friend, he promised her another servant girl, "As I have to go shortly on several campaigns against hostile Indians ... I will send another who is a little larger."

He continued to hire out adult Indians, sending thirty to Suñol on a single occasion. Suñol was to keep them as long as he liked. Sutter would allow the Indians to return to their families when Suñol was through with them.

Sutter had left his wife in Switzerland and took a mistress named Manuiki, a Hawaiian. Although Sutter had a large number of young Indian girls who were constantly at his beck and call, dearest to Sutter was Manuiki, who bore him several children, none of whom survived infancy.

○ ○ ○

Punishments dealt out by Sutter upon the Indians were sometimes harsh. One day in 1846, it was rumored that Chief Raphero had turned his *Mokelumnes* against Sutter and he was going to burn Sutter's wheat crops, and, if possible, kill Sutter himself.

Rather than await Raphero's attack, Sutter tracked Raphero and his warriors down and defeated them. The chief was captured, brought back to the fort, court-martialed, and sentenced to death. He was then speedily killed by a firing squard. Afterwards Raphero's head was cut off and impaled on a spike above the main gate of the fort. Sutter kept it up there for a long time, with long black hair hanging. Sutter said it served as a warning to those who threatened him or *Nueva Helvecia*.

During the fateful year of 1848, Sutter continued to maintain a strong hand in his relationship with the *Chucumne* Indians on the Cosumnes River. Entries from Sutter's *Nueva Helvecia Diary* read:

March 5, 1848: "Took a ride with Mr. Zins to the Cosumney Rancheria to get people to work."

March 12, 1848: "Dances in the Cosumney Rancheria."

March 13, 1848: "A good many Indians at work, but all very tired on account their dances, at 9 o'clock in the evening left with Messrs. Kyburz and Wittmer to the Cosumney Rancheria, and for not having obeyed my orders burnt their *Temascal* [sweat house]."

April 24, 1848: "Last night a dance in the Cosumney Rancheria, all the boys etc. came late in the morning—a good many was asleep instead at work, got punished for having done so."

Gold was initially discovered by James Marshall on January 24, 1848, at the Nisenan village named *Coloma* where Sutter had put up a sawmill. In February, Sutter picked up a few specimens of gold himself in the tail race of the sawmill. The first newspaper account was published March 15th in the *California* in San Francisco. The first swarm of white miners appeared in the summer months, and the town of Dry Diggings (later Placerville) was established. White ranchers along the Cosumnes River sent about one hundred *Chucumne* Indians to the Dry Diggings area, paying them fifty cents a day. It was not unusual for an Indian to dig from $50 to $100 in gold dust a day. In this way the white ranchers gathered a large sum in a short time. On the bars and other places where dirt had to be washed, Indians (such as the fifty working for Mr. John Sinclair on the North Fork) used their perfectly watertight willow baskets.

Skirmishes between the newly arrived miners (truly outsiders) versus the Maidu-Nisenan and *Chucumnes* Indians began in earnest in the fall of 1848, first at a Maidu (possibly Konkow) village along Bear River to the northwest. There, twenty-five Indian men, women and children were murdered by the miners. In the spring of 1849, Indian tribes who by then had banded together, made two retaliatory raids: one on Spanish Bar on the Middle Fork of the American, killing seven miners; the second a week later, taking the lives of five more.

The miners became incensed! A fever to exterminate "those damn Digger Indians" spread through the new village of Sacramento that had sprung up overnight, to the mining camps. Unrest reached a peak and posses of men formed, combing the hills with the sole purpose of killing *every* Indian man, woman, and child they found. Whites from Oregon were the worst, executing seven innocent natives at *Coloma*. (Accounts as to what happened heretofore to the Maidu-Nisenan are absent.) In the *Coloma* Indian village, a blanket and a hat, said to have belonged to two of the miners killed, were supposedly found. More mayhem followed.

It is recorded that white rancher William Daylor heard of the unrest and sent word for the *Chucumne* Indian families working at his claim in Dry Diggings to come back to safety, to the ranch at Sloughhouse on the Cosumnes River forthwith. There were fifty-four altogether, twenty men and thirty-four women and children. Just a few miles from safety, these unarmed *Chucumnes* were intercepted by a party of armed men who immediately began slaughtering them. Only four men escaped, running on toward Daylor's ranch. But when just in sight of the ranch buildings, the posse caught up with the four and shot three of them in the back. Daylor and his wife Sarah were eyewitnesses: the hunted Indians were so close that they could see their faces contorted with terror and exhaustion. When the leading rider's revolver fired, one of the Indians pitched headlong into the grass. Two more shots followed and two more of the Indians fell, one not thirty feet from where the Daylors stood. The fourth dashed into the sanctity of one of the outhouses. He would have been killed too, only Mr. Daylor ordered the posse off his property, threatening to kill them in return, so they left.

The gold rush days devastated the Indian Peoples. They were blown about like chaff in the wind. There is really nothing more to tell.

It was after the gold rush of 1849, which brought in so many more white strangers—and more sicknesses for the Indians (cholera, smallpox, tuberculosis)—when Tokiwa sought to talk with Sutter himself. Visions and prayers had not stopped the dying. Tokiwa heard that Sutter prized a medical book which he used to treat all the sick at the fort. If the Indian sick were still dying from a white man's disease, then perhaps it would take the white doctor's medicine to rid his people of their sicknesses. Tokiwa went to the fort with skins to trade for this book. But Sutter was not at the fort. With the gold rush invasion, Sutter was losing about everything. The lucrative gold fields were not on his property. He was gone, trying to find new workers to finish his other flour mill.

Also, in January 1850, Sutter's wife and children arrived from across the seas to live with him for a time on Sutter's Hock farm (Yuba City). Then in 1865, Sutter and his family left for good, never to return.

Many of the Indian people, however, saw Sutter for the last time in 1863, because of the Round Valley story; some as early as 1853, when taken to the first reservation at *Nome Lāckee,* about twenty miles west of the present town of Tehama.

The *wo-lese* (white men) now wanted the rich, gold land of the Indian Peoples, even where there wasn't any gold. They called *all* the California Indians "Diggers" instead of people. In three drives, the blue soldiers on horseback drove about four or five hundred Indians, mostly Maidu, across the Great Valley, past the sacred Buttes, and over the rugged Coast Range to Round Valley at Covelo, a trek of 125 miles.

The blue soldiers (called the Second Infantry of the California Volunteers) first herded several groups together into a corral in Chico. Although people came from different outfits—South People, West People, Konkow, Wailakis, Pitt Rivers—the white men treated the groups alike in complete disregard to marked areas, tribal customs, and languages. The Chico Indians did not like the West People coming into their country and poisoned many.

Then all the peoples were forced from Chico westward, out of their territories, even though many of the Indians already were sick from being rounded up, marched, and corralled. The journey was made hard. If the people had to rest, the soldiers herded them into a ditch and rested them, just like they rested stock. If they could not travel, the soldiers drove them anyway with whips. And if they fell down and did not get up, soldiers jabbed them in the rear with big knives on their guns, going "Ah, Ah, Ah." Some of the old ladies and men could not walk any farther. A lot of people tried to run off, but a lot got killed. And many were sick. When one woman carrying a baby fell, a soldier bayonetted her through the baby on her back, killing them both. Bayonets were used to conserve ammunition because soldiers had to make their own bullets.

Of the 461 Indians force-marched to Round Valley beginning September 4, 1863, only 277 reached the reservation, and most of these were sick. Only 32 were reported "killed" or "died" along the way by the soldiers. Marie Potts, a Maidu elder, told how some of the Indians were even blindfolded, put on barges, taken down the Sacramento River to the ocean, and up the coast to northern California. Many Indians stayed in Round Valley, which the Maidu called *Hokum Halte,* "Standing Quiet." But just as many escaped and returned home or there abouts.

That is the Round Valley story.

○ ○ ○

More summers passed and the white population continued to grow and spread out in all directions. All around *Kadema,* squatters, who had first come for the gold, had now turned to agriculture. Exotic plants and alien fruit trees appeared. Pear, plum, and apple orchards were planted, dotting the river fronts. Farmers settled all across the Valley. They began raising poultry, cattle, and horses. They grew hops, rice, and many kinds of vegetables. The landscape became confined with wood and barbed wire fences. New roads were cut. Railroad spurs branched out from the Central Pacific rail yards in Sacramento. The walls of Sutter's fort crumbled in disrepair, leaving only its central building. The entire fort area, including the wheat fields, were now covered with large, enduring houses filled with people. Sacramento, Folsom, and Marysville were now cities. Men in suits and ladies in long dresses walked or rode in horse drawn carriages, buggies, and trolley cars. The noise, glare, and clutter of a very different lifestyle prevailed.

Yet, headman Mike Cleanso and So-me-lah, the *Peheipe,* still led village activities and maintained an active dance house at *Kadema*. Fifteen families had stayed on and each had a one room, wood-framed dwelling. Many others had simply disappeared, taking work somewhere in the white society.

One day in 1875, thirty-six years after Sutter first came to the Native People, headman Mike Cleanso told his son "Blind" Tom (who became blind from a disease when he was eight years old), that he and So-me-lah had decided to journey to visit Tokiwa who lived in a house just outside of Yuba City adjacent the Buttes. "We want to see that the old man is all right; to see if he should stay by himself any longer," So-me-lah explained. They said good-bye to their wives and families and left, taking a wagon pulled by two horses.

Tokiwa was very glad to see them. This elder, who was now 94 years old, had many wrinkles across his face and his hair was as white as the first *Ku'ksū* man of ancient times. Tokiwa had earned the reputation of a powerful healer and inspirational prophet. He was also a respected orator.

"I'm getting close to death," Tokiwa said slowly. "I'm alone and sometimes my heart really aches." Tokiwa then stood up, and touched his eyes with one hand.

"I carry a terrible burden; that I survived and so many of the others did not. Why did I survive?" he asked. Mike Cleanso and So-me-lah looked at each other, feeling sad.

"My doctoring has told me about death. I've done the right things. I'm strong today because of our way. The way we were raised. My medicine has given me the strength through these years to keep going. We had a way that worked and I can see that the white man, he has a way too. Not all bad. He has wheat just as we had our acorn crop. We both store our food. We had Nature's orchards. They collect gold and silver coins just as we collected clam shell beads.

"Yet, I don't understand the white man's greed; his

ruthlessness. Why does the white man take a rifle and just shoot at a Nisenan just for the sake of it? We Nisenan, you know, always liked outsiders. We would be entertained and we learned things then. But these outsiders broke from our code. They judge another based merely on skin color. They don't fight war as ceremony. Where is their *hudessi* who can dodge arrows? Where is their Secret Society *Yĕ'poni* to show boys how to become men?

"The whites destroy the land. They so muddy our streams that they kill the fish, and the clams suffocate from all the silt. The great acorn trees that are gifts from the Creator for all the people for all the seasons, they chop down to make way for roads and fields.

"All people need open eyes. White people cannot begin to understand the Indian until they begin to understand our way as we see it. Now more than ever people need to have open eyes to other ways of living. If they are ever wise, they can learn from us.

"But we have faults too. Why do some of our people deny they are Nisenan? Many have disappeared. I had one friend who works as a cowboy, and he doesn't recognize me anymore.

"I feel sorry for any man who tries to learn another way. He then has two customs, two teachers, two ways. Sometimes these ways talk to them in the dark, and then madness is very near."

"What of the future, Tokiwa?" asked Mike Cleanso. "What is going to happen?"

"Our world in a sense is ending," Tokiwa said. "But the world is not yet at an end. Our people will come back, and will raise up the sacred ways again.

"Everything, every animal, and every person has a purpose. The Creator has chosen to send the white man to us and we must learn to work with him while keeping our old ways strong.

"To live up to the Creator's purpose, every person has the power of self-control, and that's where spiritual power begins. When this is practiced, the time will be right for more revelations. The Creator will come again and spiritual power will again return to this land."

This was the very last speech Tokiwa made to his people. Soon after Tokiwa had gone to bed, he died in his sleep. All the Indian people greatly mourned him, as his heart climbed the feather rope back to Earth-Maker, the Creator.

1903 and 1932

The Falling-Leaf Season

14. "Blind" Tom Cleanso, One of the Last

"I am the only one, the only one left.
An old man, I carry the gambling-board;
An old man, I sing the gambling song.
The roots I eat of the Valley.
The pepper-ball is round.
The water trickles, trickles.
The water-leaves grow along the river bank.
I run the hand, I wiggle the tail.
I am a doctor, I am a doctor."

Konkow Maidu

C. Hart Merriam wrote:

"In September 1903, while searching for Indians in the vicinity of Buena Vista Peak in Amador County, I visited Ione, Jackson, and neighboring localities and finally located an old Indian named Casus Oliver. He was a friendly old man and told me much concerning the early inhabitants.

"I asked if he had ever heard of *Pusuni*, an old *rancheria* which I had learned from other Indians had been situated on the north side of the American River near its junction with the Sacramento.

"I had been told that the inhabitants of *Pusuni*

had been extinct for many years, but old Oliver assured me that they were not all dead yet, stating that a full blood old woman from that *rancheria* had married a *Kanaka* who worked on the Sacramento River levees and was then living in a houseboat anchored in the Sacramento opposite the mouth of the American River.

"Going to Sacramento and following the east bank of the river northward, I saw the houseboat anchored as described. In answer to my call, a girl came up on deck, untied a small rowboat, and took me over. On asking for her mother, she said her mother was not at home, that she had gone to see her old blind brother* then living near the old Hop Ranch, about nine miles up the American River.

"During later visits at the houseboat, I succeeded in obtaining from the mother a very interesting vocabulary which I had every reason to believe was the language of the *Pusuni.* But at the end of my last visit she became greatly disturbed and finally broke down and told me that the language she had given me was not that of *Pusuni* but of the *No'to-muse,* a Maidu tribe of the mainland some distance east. On asking if anyone were still alive who could talk the language of *Pusuni,* she replied, "Only one, my brother,* "Blind" Tom.' He, as just mentioned, lived a little north of the American River, about nine miles from Sacramento.

"Guided by her directions, I drove to the Southern Pacific railroad station at Ben Ali, and thence easterly for some miles through open fields. Arriving at the place indicated, I found old man Tom, living in a small cabin with a Negro woman.

---

* "Brother" is apparently used here as an endearment. "Blind" Tom was actually her nephew; refer to Appendix H, Cleanso Family Geneology.

He was totally blind and was the most bashful person I have ever known, speaking in a low, hesitating voice, obviously much embarrassed. Still, I made a beginning, and in the course of subsequent visits (at intervals until he disappeared circa 1932), I succeeded in obtaining a fairly full vocabulary of his language, which he invariably called *Nis-se Pa-we-nan.*"

○ *Circa 1932* ○

A tremor of fear and sadness reflected in Tom's voice as he prepared to leave the place of his birth. So many memories were capsulated inside this living Nisenan man.

"I am the last one. I am the last survivor of the *No'-to-muse* left who lives here at *Kadema.* The other *Nisena-ne* have gone.

"But Paméla and Lillie Williams, my cousin, worry that I can't get around here alone and feed myself. They live in Broderick, in a houseboat anchored on the Big River opposite *Pusuni.* Any day they're coming to take me to live with them. Guess they'll want me back in Oakland for a spell, at the Home for the Blind.

"I told Lillie I got to stay and die here at *Kadema* to close the circle, for it is here where I was born—here where I can talk with woodpecker and mockingbird. But I'm trouble for everybody I suppose, living here alone, now that my wife, Lizzie Terry is gone.

"I can't see, of course. Been blind since I was very little. I saw only for eight years. And now, I can't hear well neither. But I still like it here and I want to stay.

"The others in my family and from my village have already left. They left long ago and they've changed. I can tell 'cause when some of them come by to visit, they don't speak *Nisena-ne* any more, and their children don't think or act the way the old people did when they were little. These children use their mouths more than their ears. Even after they grow up, they never sit still long enough to hear God as we did.

"We obeyed God, and at night and in the daytime, we talked to God in our hearts and asked everything of God.

"We don't get the things we ask for at once. After one year or two years—then we get what we asked for.

"That we believe, that is our God.

"In the old days the old people told us like that, when *we* were children, teaching us. That is our religion even though we don't make speeches to God in a house; the old people taught us. 'I know that,' they said.

"I'm the only one left who knows the whole *Niseana-ne* tongue and the old ways. That's why all those anthropologists come to see me and ask questions. They worked with me at the university and while I was close by at the Home for the Blind.

"When I'm gone, no one will have it. I'm the last one. All my life I want back our good old ways at *Kadema*. But I guess I can never have it. I'm a very old *Nisena-ne*. I'm 80 years now.

"But I have a secret. I return to the old ways in my dreams. Bet *you* don't know that. You don't listen to your dreams so you don't know how to.

"I think about the early days. There were lots of family around. My father was Captain 'Mike' Cleanso who worked for Sutter. My father was the last chief at *Kadema*. Before he died in 1901, he became one of the richest chiefs around. He had sixteen bearskins and two or three trunks full of beads and shells. My father is buried right here.

"Delores Cleanso was my mother. She died before my father in 1893, and is buried here at *Kadema* also. My mother came from *Yukulme*, a Valley *Nisena-ne* village on the lower Feather River up north. She talked a little different than my father—a different language. The anthropologists call it a different dialect.

"My father had two sisters. His elder sister died long ago. She was over one hundred ten years old when she died. She's buried at *Pusuni*. His younger sister was Paméla Cleanso Adams, my aunt. She and her *Kanaka* husband lived with us at *Kadema*.

"My father moved to *Kadema* from *Pusuni* and became headman after headman Tawec died. When my father died, maybe I would have been made chief, since normally these things are passed on through blood. But I was blind and chiefs can't be blind. So when my father died things became very serious. This was when almost everyone left. Our village life was over. A lot of the people left to work as ranch hands and farm laborers. I worked at the hop ranch on the south side of our river, making a little money. That was the work we did then.

"Even though I'm blind, I've always been pretty good with my hands. I've worked with stone, shell, and wood a lot. Abalone money paid pretty good.

"I used to make wooden mortars from the forks of oak trees. I would burn out the parts of the tree. We used them with stone pestles to pound out acorns.

"I live in this shack with tarpaper roof, nothing like the houses kept by the old people. My father told me he remembered two dance houses at *Kadema*.

"I use a horse-drawn plow to cultivate four acres. I plant potatoes. I also used the plow to conceal the burials. White folks come again and again. They look for grave goods. They dig big holes in our cemetery. They've even done this while we were living here. They even stole the headstones. So I plowed the area over and now they can't find the graves at all.

"My father, Captain 'Mike' Cleanso, told me many things that happened before I was born. He mentioned over and over again several names of people he knew or heard about when he was very young. He remembered Big

Meadows and Big Matos as great hunters. So-se-yah-mah was a great dance captain at *Kadema*. Hunchup was a medicine man. There were other names and stories my father could recall while talking on through the night.

"There was the time when Captain Sutter came to Sacramento and built the fort. Sutter brought with him the *Kanakas* who married into my family. Some of them settled at *Kadema* permanently and worked as *vaqueros* for Captain Sutter. They and their children are also buried here.

"Another time my father and his older sister were kidnapped. They went to pick blackberries beyond the marsh along the river. The enemy happened to come across them. They were kidnapped and taken to the south country, the country south of Mt. Diablo.

"They stayed there about four years, my father said. His sister kept taking away all kinds of food and hiding it, little by little. When they ran away, they took the food.

"They came on the east side of Mt. Diablo. When they came to the water, they made a boat out of tule and crossed.

"Later they came to a river. Using the boat again, they went up the river thinking it might be their river. They actually went up the Cosumnes.

"The next morning, his sister told my father to climb a tree to look around. When he had climbed to the top of the tree, he saw trees stretching in a black line. He told her what he saw. Maybe it was the river they were looking for.

"He climbed down and they went on. They went along for about five or six days. Once in a while they even traveled at night. Finally when they came to their river, they went straight towards *Kadema*.

"When they got there they shouted across to the camp. The people heard them and came out to see who they were. Tawec and the others recognized them and everyone started crying and laughing. They were really happy, and had a 'small time.'

"Blind" Tom Cleanso.[*]

"My father and aunt could speak the Lower Country language, a Miwok dialect. They had been there four years and had learned the language."

(Tom now paused, but more memories stayed with him.)

"I remember the smell of acorn soup cooking and deer meat frying on summer evenings.

"I remember that black acorns were the best. The Mountain People even traded their salt, fish, and basket grass for some of our black acorns. I remember when Paméla and my father walked all the way to the coast with burden baskets filled with acorns just to trade to the Coast People for shells.

"I remember we'd swim in the river and the sun would bake us on the peaceful sandy beaches.

"And later I remember when my younger relatives felt embarrassed when I continued to sing my songs. But I sing them still anyway.

"The old people at *Pusuni* and *Kadema* are gone now. All the people there are gone. But some say the present world will be torn up.

"Lillie's coming now. *Uk'o'yim ni,* I'm going. Goodbye."

O O O

"Blind" Tom Cleanso died circa 1932 when he was over eighty years old. Exactly when and where he is buried are unknown.

---

[*] Courtesy of the R.H. Lowie Museum of Anthropology, U.C. Berkeley.

Captain "Mike" Cleanso (Grimšo), the last headman at Kadema, who also worked for Sutter. Here at age 100 plus, circa 1900.

"Mike" Cleanso and wife Dolores.

Paméla Cleanso Adams, sister of Mike Cleanso (1834—1934).

Lillie Williams, cousin of "Blind" Tom, with reporter.

1984

June

15. Going To A Big Time—The Bear Dance

"Before the present race of Indians, it is believed that the bears were human beings and went around wild."

Joe Marine

In the month of June when the trees bend over all laden with fruit, the age-old *Wa-dom Buh-yee,* the Bear Dance of the Mountain Maidu once again is celebrated at the ranch of Gladys Mankins. Held in the pine forest and mountain meadow country at the base of 8,000 foot Thompson Peak near Janesville, Lassen County, California; the ceremony is little advertised, but is open to the public.

On June 9, 1984, I took Highway 80 to Reno, and then Highway 395 north to Janesville. A wooden sign with a painted blue arrow read, "Bear Dance," and led to a small grassy meadow surrounded by tall pine trees. I parked on the Mankins' ranch property alongside the several other vehicles which had already arrived. The crowd was mainly north-central California Indians, many full-blood, who had come from miles around. They were busy talking and laughing with friends, gambling, preparing foods, and selling their crafts.

The Indian people are survivors, I thought to myself. They have the Coyote spirit inside them. In spite of wars and plagues, they live—and they always will. They are back to raise up the sacred Indian ways. Although much has changed and been lost, the Maidu-Nisenan are strong and have never given up. They have kept their identities and their purpose—their way of life.

I looked intently throughout the crowd, for the day became a link to the past. Is there somewhere here another Tokiwa? I pondered.

Here are the things I learned that day from the Bear Dance ceremonies, that help guide Indians throughout life.

Everyone wants to go to the Bear Dance. They will lose power if they stay away. People have a good time—they eat, they gamble, and they dance and sing all night, as they commune with the spirits of the land.

In the morning, when the rising sun rays touch the dance ground, a man carries the grizzly bear hide. Bear skitters over the dance area, hardly touching the ground. Marvin Potts, a recent leader, takes the bearskin and hangs it on a curved willow pole on the edge of the ceremonial ground. On a second pole is hung tassels made from the inner bark of the maple, with orange stripes made from the dye of crushed bark of the alder to imitate the rattlesnake.

The old-timers stand in front of the hide. They calm the bear by tying bundles of wormwood onto the hide. Then they speak whatever comes from their heart. They talk to the spirits in the sacred lakes of the Sierras, to the spirits in the sacred mountains shaped like sweathouses, to the spirits in the land beneath them.

The Bear Dance marks the coming of a new year. So at the beginning of the year, the people dance with a bear hide and the rattlesnake flag. To keep a bear hide, the old-timers had to talk mighty nice to the bear, hang the hide out where everybody could see it and preach to it. If they didn't that bear hide was liable to kill them.

The bear is held in great awe and respect. Before the

"Rattlesnake and Bear." Photographs by Richard Burrill this chapter.

Bear Dance. Left to right: "Spirit dancers;" Marvin Potts, Joe Marine, Craig LaPena, and Marvin Marine.

present race of Indians, it was believed that the bears were human beings who were wild and had hair on their bodies. They once were *Yĕ'poni*, members of the Secret Society, and now are too sacred to be touched. Therefore, these bears are never molested in any way by the Hill Maidu.

The bear cubs understand everything, regardless of what language is spoken. They must be fed clean food. When they die, they are buried with shells and beads—"like a person."

Later in the day someone uncovers the barbeque pit and lifts out the deer meat. Everyone then eats greens and potatoes, salmon and deer, and, of course, acorn soup.

Afterwards more dancers performed. The men wore salmon-orange colored flicker headbands, moving their heads from side to side. The women danced with their left hand on their hip and their right hand waving a scarf in front of them. Later the people held hands in great concentric circles and danced. They wore worm-wood stalks that hung around their head and over their faces.

Maidu speaker Joe Marine, who is the *Pahno* (grizzly bear) this year, steps before the people and speaks:

"The Bear Dance is not for just one person. It is for all of us. It marks the coming of a new year. If you feel good this weekend, then you will feel good all this year. My dancing has helped me realize there is meaning to life.

"Open your ears and listen.

"Open your hearts and understand.

"Respect yourself. Understand yourself. Do this not for today but do this for the children. The children are our backup system and we are their stepping stones. This life is real. Take care of yourself and know your path in life."

Joe Marine continued speaking, "The reason for the Bear Dance is that every year we have to calm bear and rattlesnake down or we are apt to be bitten.

"The World-Maker came down before us. He understood everything.

"Rattlesnake came over. He said, 'I am the most dangerous thing.' Then World-Maker threw acorn bread on his head to stop rattlesnake. World-Maker stepped on rattlesnake's head and this is why the rattlesnake has a flat head with a diamond mark.

"Grizzly bear arrived saying, 'I am the most powerful here on Earth. I don't have to listen to this man.' Then grizzly bear turned away and the Creator pinched off his long tail, and that is why bear has a short tail to this day. Rattlesnake and *Pahno* then hid out in the woods and that is why we still have two dangerous animals.

"This is what the Bear Dance is all about. The children need us. They look at us, 'Is this the way we're going to be?' they ask. Live good! Because this is our way. We came from the earth and we'll go on to the next world. Understand or people won't feel good.

"Join hands! The circle has no beginning and no end. When the last day comes, you get in a circle so we can go on to the next world."

Joe now walked over to the willow pole supporting the bearskin and the maple tassel flag. Flagman Marvin Potts helped his cousin Joe get inside the bear hide to become bear. Marvin carried the flag.

Flagman Marvin Potts warned the people, "Don't beat the bear. Rub the bear with wormwood. That is good! Treat the bear with respect. They are sacred. Never make fun of the skin, regardless of how shabby it may look. *Pahno* will hear you, and he will go against you.

"Follow *Pahno* around the dance area. Now follow him to the creek. Rub him with stalks of wormwood. There

Joe Marine strokes bear with wormwood during Bear Dance.

Joe Marine as bear in Bear Dance. Flagman Marvin Potts holds willow pole.

everyone throw wormwood into the creek. Wash yourself with wormwood and water. Pray for your cousins who are sick this year. Wash and pray.

"This is good. Break up the flag now," Marvin continued. "Let the maple tassels of the rattlesnake flag float down the creek. Don't touch them. Let them go. Wash with wormwood so your prayers will be answered. That is the old way. That is good."

1986

Epilogue

"When you leave this earth, you leave through Spirit Mountain."

Maidu Informant

As a result of my studies of the Maidu-Nisenan Indians, I found myself possessed with a great wish to survey the Buttes myself. As the Buttes were the site of the beginning of the Maidu, it made sense that these Indians believed that when a person died, his spirit went to back to the Buttes, which they called Spirit Mountain.

Now the Buttes are on private property. I discovered that an archaeologist named Peter M. Jensen had surveyed the Buttes as part of his doctoral thesis. Carefully, I read through Jensen's papers and discovered that he had mostly surveyed parts of West Butte and North Butte of the mountain range. There was nothing specifically mentioned about South Butte, which is the tallest peak and, to me, most looks like an assembly dance house. Jensen stated that he had found a complete lack of burials within the Buttes. Two sites though, were of some interest. One site in the West Butte area had eight caves, but all were void of any evidence of Indian occupation. Another site, located north of North Butte, had mysterious petroglyphs in the form of pitted boulders. "This particular Indian rock-art," Jensen writes:

"... confirmed to an ancient and widespread petro-glyph style, which appears to be found over most of western North America. Among the neighboring Shasta Indians (and perhaps the Hupa, Tolowa, and Karok as well) they served as "rain rocks." Cere-monies were performed at or near them to cause rain to fall or to make it stop falling. It is possible that the pitted boulder may represent a ceremonial attempt to halt the rain or flood waters within the northern Sacramento Valley by a group who had been forced out of their village by rising waters.

"An entirely different contention is that the pitted boulders served as 'baby rocks' that were pecked out by women, as was customary of Pomo Indian women who were desirous of conceiving children."

Of these pitted boulders at the Sutter Buttes, only fifty objects of "aesthetic achievement" were found so far, belonging to those peoples who occupied the Buttes (either Northwestern Maidu or River Patwin). These petroglyphs were of a possible subsistence, fertility nature or about some aspect of magico-religious life.

Overall, Jensen had discovered several occupation sites, temporary camps, quarry-workshops, rock shelters and caves, and several bedrock mortar sites. Articles of significance uncovered were stone pendants, quartz crystals, minute quantities of red ochre, and some recent glass trade beads.

In March of 1986, my wish came true. I surveyed the Buttes. I had the pleasure of being led on a one-day hike by Mr. Ira Heinrich, a sensitive man who has spent much of his life studying the Buttes as a place of historical and spiritual power. One morning I met Ira at the parking lot of Munger's Market in the community of Sutter. We drove to the Dean's place, which lies just inside the Buttes, stopping several times to pass through a series of road gates. We were afforded a very clear day without any rain clouds in sight.

Upon approaching the mountain range, I was impressed by the isolation of the Buttes from the other mountains and their sharp contrast to the surrounding flatness of the Valley. This called to mind one local legend I had heard. The Great Spirit, after forming the Sierra Nevada range to the east and the Coast Range to the west, dusted off his hands and paused to rest while contemplating his creations. Where the dust fell is where the Buttes now stand.

The trailhead started from behind the Dean's ranch house. The hike began with a gradual ascent along a dirt road which followed a creek. We took a refreshing rest by a small creek bed.

Ira explained how, geologically, the Buttes were volcanic in orgin. This accounted for the abruptness with which they appear in the Valley. Volcanic activity began with slow intrusions into older sedimentary beds during Pliocene time. Volcanic activity became explosive during the Pleistocene epoch between 1.5 and 2 million years ago.

Anyone of these Buttes, I thought, could be the great dance lodge of the dead. I remembered the references in the Maidu creation story and that, by custom, doors were normally built on the west side. All these things I wanted to investigate.

The ascent, for the most part, was a gradual one, during which time we sighted several animals. Besides the cows and many types of birds and several ground squirrels, we saw a black-tail deer on a ridge above us. I was especially moved when a golden eagle's nest was sighted, resting on a craggy cliff above us. A pair of golden eagles lifted skyward and preceded to glide on the healthy air currents around the Buttes.

The ascent to the ridgeline took most of the day. Unfortunately, none of the many places I searched yielded any secrets. The landscape seemed to offer innumerable possibilities I didn't have time to explore. No new petroglyphs nor pitted boulders were discovered. There were no hidden caves nor "magic" rocks found, nor doorways discovered through which I could "go inside" and contact the spirits.

The final climb to the top of the Buttes involved a kind of cross-country hiking on grassy slopes dotted by rock outcrops. The top view provided us a spectacular, panoramic vista west to the Coast Range and the Sierra Nevada to the east. Below, the checkerboard pattern of the Valley farmland surrounding the Buttes resembled a patchwork carpet which led to the foothills of each mountain range. Even Mt. Shasta, about 160 miles to the north and especially sacred to the neighboring Wintu and Shasta Indians, was clearly visible.

I gazed down from one of the mountain tops... possibly eagle's camp... from this roundhouse of the dead where a person goes when he dies. Way down there somewhere, on the Valley floor I searched for Tokiwa, for some connection with this Nisenan man.

Suddenly, a lone coyote appeared from deep in the landscape. Neither total sinner or saint, I sensed that I stood before the Coyote Spirit who had never left; who rules the entire world to this day, together, yet side by side the benevolent and wise Creator.

Chapter Notes

"He knows most about the world who knows best that world which is within his own footsteps.

Not all hills and valleys are alike, but unless a man knows his own hills and valleys he is not likely to understand those of another..."

Hal Borland

Introduction

☐ An estimated **76,000 California Indians** were living in the Sacramento Valley in prehistoric times, according to Sherburne F. Cook's *Populations of the California Indians 1769-1970*, (1976, 19, 42; UC Press, Berkeley). If we add the thinly populated northern tier of tribes, 9,600 ... we get for the entire northern interior 85,700 persons on 35,500 square miles.

☐ Evidence that neighboring Chucumnes were the Nisenan's **bitter enemies** comes from Heinrich Lienhard (1941, 7).

☐ Headman **Tawec's** name (Kroeber 1929, 264).

Chapter One

☐ **Fictional embellishments** are used only in parts of the story for the sole purpose of bringing to life again these Indian cultures.

☐ **Maidu,** pronounced my-doo; derived from the Maidu word for "man," *maiduk*. Stephen Powers (1877) first used Maidu as a descriptive label for these Indians, who live in north-central California.

☐ **Nisenan** is used in reference to the people who occupied the Southern Maidu area. *Na-n* means "side," literally "our tribelet"—"Indian" as apart from white men; those "among us," according to Uldall and Shipley (1966, 86). In contrast, ethnographer John Duncan III reports that "Nisenan" was a name given these Indians by the white man. Informant Lizzie Enos told Duncan that *"Tankus"* was the term other Maidu groups used to describe the Southern Maidu people (Duncan 1961, 6). *"Tanku"* is also the Patwin name for the Nisenan town at the mouth of the Feather River, which would make it *Wolok* or *Woolock* or *Ole* according to another informant (Kroeber 1932, 268).

☐ The **Creation myth** that follows is a composite of several Maidu sources transcribed over the years from a number of Maidu informants. Parts have been adapted from Richard Simpson's *Ooti: A Maidu Legacy* by written permission of the author and the publisher, Celestial Arts in Berkeley, California. Other sources include: Roland B. Dixon, *The Huntingon California Expedition: Maidu Myths* 1902, 39-45; Don M. Chase, *People of the Valley: The Concow Maidu*, Sebastopol.

California, pp. 33-46. Kroeber wrote that, "The Valley Maidu... seem to have developed the fullest creation mythology of any Sacramento Valley people." (1932, 407)

☐ Among the Nisenan, Stephen Powers cites the myth in which Moon was the first thing in existence and Coyote the second. **Moon and Coyote** created all things, including man (Loeb 1932-34, 158; Powers 1877, 341).

☐ Both Leland Scott, a 74-year old northwestern Foothill Maidu and ethnographer C. Hart Merriam reported more stories about the **first acorn tree.** Merriam was told that the precise location of this sacred tree was on the west side of Butte Creek half a mile east of the city of Durham and on the south side of the road. *Ta'doiko* was the ancient name of this location where the village pronounced *Es'kenne* existed into recent times.

Merriam recorded this about the first tree: "In the long ago the first land was at Durham. Here grew an oak tree which bore all kinds of acorns—acorns of the valley oak, live oak, and others. This tree was cut by whites a few years ago when clearing for the railroad. After this, many of our people died." (Chico, 1919).

Leland Scott told Dorothy Hill this related account: "At Durham there was an oak tree standing for a long, long time. It was put there by the Creator to give food to the Indians. On this tree there was one limb of black oak, one limb of white oak, one limb of mountain oak, one limb of live oak, and one limb of blue oak. It was loaded every fall when the acorns were needed. If there were no acorns around here (Cherokee), the people knew where to go to get the acorns. They could go to Durham and get all they wanted. The tree was a great big oak—as big as a redwood.

"White men wanted to cut it down to put a school house there. To them the tree was in the way. This tree was put there for Indians only. The Indians said, 'If the white men cut the tree down, what will we eat?' The white men went to work and cut it down. When it was almost cut down, but the tree was still standing, blood started coming out of it, flowing like water.

" 'What kind of tree are we cutting down?' asked a white man. The old Indians knew what kind of tree the white men were cutting down, but they didn't tell. The Indians just kept their mouths shut.

"So the white men kept on sawing, sawing, and the blood kept running out like blood from a stuck hog. As the men were afraid the tree might fall the wrong way, they waited until morning to finish cutting it. The next morning they came and found the tree was on the ground, but no one knew how it had fallen. There had been no noise—nothing. The night had been quiet. The white men said it fell by itself during the night, so they were not responsible for cutting it down." (C. Hart Meriam 1966, 315; and Dorothy Hill 1969).

☐ **South Butte** of the Sutter (Marysville) Buttes stands 2,132 feet, the highest.

☐ Northeastern Maidu informant Herb Young credits Little Lizard with giving mankind **five fingers** (Rathbun, *Sun, Moon*, 1973, 48).

☐ Ku'ksū and Morning-Star Woman are Konkow Maidu names. The Nisenan name for the **first man** was *Aikut* and the **first woman,** *Yototowi*. (Powers 1877, 339).

Chapter Two

☐ **Yamanködö** village name and location was told Anna Gayton by "Blind" Tom Cleanso who stated "upstream other side *Kadema*, below *Utcup* and *Ekwo*, still farther upstream" (Gayton 1925, *Bancroft Library Notes*).

☐ **Secret societies** were prevalent among the Maidu and Patwin and not with the Nisenan (Gardner 1977, 23).

☐ The Valley Nisenan (Southern Maidu) had one **Secret Society** organization. *Yĕ'poni* is the Maidu word for "fully initiated dancer," while the Nisenan word for "initiate" is *temeya* (Loeb 1932-34, 189).

☐ **Women** were not actual members of the Society, although certain women were instructed in dancing, afterwards becoming the dance leaders for the women. The men danced inside the dance house, the women outside (Loeb 1932-34, 169).

☐ Playing **football,** (Shipley and Uldall 1966, 91).

☐ The title "Chief" was virtually non-existent among California Indians. **"Headman"** is the more proper term to use. Yet, because Chief appears in later translations and writings, Chief is used occasionally in this story as well. But this is not done to ignore earlier traditions.

☐ **Three realms of power;** read Bean (1975, 58, 62).

☐ **Star constellations** recognized included *Ku-le-yo-tik* or the Three Girls and One Boy (Big Dipper) cited in Beals (1933, 357) and *yotcok* or the Seven Sisters (the Pleiades) and spelled *Oto*, the seven stars in Chapter Five of this book (Kroeber 1929, 286).

☐ **Unai**—Beals (1933, 384). Perhaps *Unai* is allied to the Plateau Shoshonean "water baby" called *Paxwa*. (Gifford 1927, 247). Read also James Downs, *The Two Worlds of the Washo* (1966, 58, 62).

☐ **Wood spirit** called *ku'ksū* (Gifford 1927, 227, 247).

☐ **Salmon's nose** cooked in ashes (Uldall and Shipley 1966, 73).

☐ **Greenish-blue** pigment (Dixon 1905, 221).

☐ Game **ama-ty** (Uldall and Shipley 1966, 90).

☐ In Maidu families, a **child might be named** after a deceased relative one year after the death, as this would remove the taboo placed on saying the dead person's name (Dixon 1905, 230-231; Loeb 1932-34, 170).

☐ The **Mona or Washo** were occasionally hostile towards the Maidu-Nisenan. Pai-u-ti called *Moan-au-zi* said also to be troublesome (Powers 1877, 320).

☐ Hole in antler **arrow straightener** (Uldall and Shipley 196, 75).

☐ **Deer neck leather.** Ibid. p. 34.

☐ Boys ornamented in dancing regalia and given a wand, **yokoli.** (Loeb 1932-34, 168).

☐ **Tested with arrows** (Uldall and Shipley 1966, 119).

☐ **Number four sacred:** Dances usually lasted four nights (Uldall and Shipley, 1966, 107, 133, 141); a dance consisted of four parts and four rounds or repetitions made up one part; they sang four songs by the drum (p. 105); "Before going home after having shot a bear, the hunters shouted four times" (p. 83); "The doctors walked round in a circle in opposite directions four times" (p. 79); "The Nisenan

bathed four mornings at dawn when the moon was dead [new moon]" (p. 113).
Kroeber (1932, 376) cites the "four directions:" "Before the first *Yombasi* initiation
there is a prayer to the four directions."

Why four is sacred may be answered because of its prevalent use by the
Creator. For instance, in the creation story the earthen pebble had grown as large as
the world when the Creator gazed upon the pebble the fourth time.

Since the Creator had created everything in fours, it was considered that man
should do all that he can in that increment. There are four periods in the life of a
human being, for instance, babyhood, childhood, adulthood, and old age. There are
four parts in everything that grows from the earth: the roots, the stem, the leaves,
and the fruit.

☐ Loeb (1932-34, 192) states about the Chico Maidu that "The boys when first
introduced into the dance-house were called **waiyomsa,** when introduced to
apprenticeship in the Society by the first initiation they were called **yombasi,** and
upon attaining full membership they became **Yĕ'poni**."

☐ **Tawec's speech** partly taken from the speech in "Legend of Oankoitupeh,"
given by *Ko-doyampeh,* the World-Maker, who was also called *Woan-no-mih,*
explaining the precepts of the religion which they were to receive from this *Ko-
doyampeh* (Powers 1877, 304).

☐ The Hill Maidu Konkow's **Creator** was named *Wo-nomi* and was also refered
to as Earth-Maker the Flaming God. *Aikat* is the Nisenan or Southern Maidu
pronunciation for Creator, also referred to as Earth-Initiate. *Ko-Doyapen* is the
Northeast Mountain Maidu word for the Creator.

☐ Powers (1877, 340) spelling is **Aikat** versus *Ajkat* as given by Uldall and
Shipley (1966, 135).

☐ **Property** that was counted were such as bearskins, beads, etc.

Chapter Three

☐ **Hunting** methods (Uldall and Shipley 1966, 145).
☐ **Manzanita stump** story (Duncan III 1963, 18-19).
☐ Hunting **rabbits** is taken from Gardner (1977, 37).
☐ Maidu Louis Kelly (**Lalook**) was from Nevada City, California, born in 1885.

Chapter Four

☐ Especially the Konkow regarded the first **salmon catch** of the season as an
occasion for ceremony (Dixon 1905, 198) as it is assumed to be true of the Nisenan
along the American River.

☐ No dugout **canoes** or tule balsas were used by the Nisenan (Gifford 1927,
252). However Kroeber (1929, 260) describes the log boat.

☐ **Richest** chiefs had many bearskins (Uldall and Shipley 1966, 174).

☐ **Wife loaning** was common between friendly groups (Beals 1933, 373).

☐ In monetary equivalents, it was reported by Stephen Powers (1877, 335), that **$100 worth of shell-money** . . . would represent two women (though Maidu never bought their wives), or two grizzly-bear skins, or 25 cinnamon-bear skins, or about three average ponies (historical times).

☐ **Hunting grizzly** (Rathbun 1973, 9-18). Last living grizzly in California was seen in 1924 in Sequoia National Park (Jewell 1987, 135).

☐ **Bear doctor** outfits (Beals 1933, 391-392).

☐ **Esto-Yamani** is where the souls of deceased persons lingered for four days. (Voegeline 1942, 119-341).

☐ Only spirits of bad people would **fail to go to heaven.** (Robert Elsasser 1980, 211-212).

☐ **Disposal of dead** (Beals 1933, 376). Nisenan always burned the dead until whites stopped this custom. When they were forced to bury instead, the Indians believed disease was caused—because gophers dug to the bodies, allowing evaporations to escape and thus transmission of diseases to occur.

☐ Doctors could see the **dead go north** from the pyre (Kroeber 1929, 265).

☐ If a Maidu had a **grudge** against a person, sometimes the grizzly-man would ambush him and slash him with the knives on his elbows.

☐ An **animal skin** automatically went to the hunter who made the first good hit. He then would give the bearskin to the chief who, in turn, would reward the hunter with valuables, namely, olivella beads, small round clamshell beads (the more valuable ones).

☐ The **Pusuni village** was located at the mouth of the American River where it empties into the Sacramento. Today, Discovery Park is on the north side. *Pusuni* was approximately ten miles downstream from *Kadema* village. In 1934, *Pusuni* (Pujune) was recorded as CA-Sac-31.

Chapter Five

☐ Kroeber was told by Nisenan informant "Blind" Tom Cleanso, that the "cry" or **"second mourning"** ceremony was called the *he-i-pai* and was held in summer (Kroeber 1929, 272).

☐ The **widows paid for a "string"** with beads, furs and food. At the end of five years, these "string" necklaces would have to be returned. (Dixon 1905, 246).

☐ Quote "You must not go **sleeping with all and sundry** any more." Taken from Uldall and Shipley (1966, 135).

☐ To **divorce,** a woman simply returned to her parents. (Beals 1933, 372).

☐ He finished these admonitions with a friendly, **"He iiiii!"** (Kroeber 1929, 265).

☐ She was both a **sucking (curing) doctor** and a **dream (religion) doctor.** Loeb (1932-1933, 159). The sucking doctor often diagnosed by feeling, then sucked at the area of pain, and removed the offending object. This could be a dead fly, a clot of blood, or a small bone or stone which he took from his mouth and showed; then buried immediately. (Kroeber 1929, 274).

☐ "Heart" meaning spirit. **Female doctors** were known to be primarily malevolent and caused great trouble with their numerous poisonings. (Dixon 1905, 267-283). "She knew how to shoot a person with "poison sticks" called *sila.*" Gifford (1927, 244).

☐ **Cá-win** or **"poisons,"** used to kill people. Patwin arrows were poisoned with the body of a white spider. So strong was the spider poison, that a half-inch puncture would kill a deer. (Kroeber 1932, 280). If a man knows a poison root and takes the proper preventive medicine, he can dig it out. One such kind is called *hokpol;* it is potato-like and red. Another is a bird, *la-lakco,* like a goose but many-colored, that sometimes got caught in duck nets. A water poison comes from *wálistcak,* which also looks like a bird. A man spearing salmon might see one, spear, kill, and keep it to kill people with; but he must take medicine to protect himself before using it. (Kroeber 1929, 275).

☐ "That tree over there or the **wind could kill you** if it wanted to." (Beals 1933, 379).

☐ Casting of **"images" of the dead** is mainly a Mountain Maidu tradition.

☐ **Ku-kini-busdi,** meaning "spirit or ghost stays within," (Kroeber 1929, 272; Hendrix 1971, 6).

☐ Some say **red, white, and black** form the most brilliant harmony in existence. They were, indeed, the most used colors by California Indians and were throughout much of North America for that matter (with yellow the fourth most used color).

The sacredness of these colors can be judged by their frequent use in the sacred dances and in war. It follows that the eagle, the white goose, red-headed woodpecker, and flicker bird merited special status.

☐ **Whistles** were made of sandhill crane bones and out of *antai,* a red-barked shrub (Gifford 1927, 241). "He gave forth unbroken whistle blasts from alternating sucking and blowing of his breath." (Powers 1877, 324).

☐ "The **women danced** where they stood, alternately raising and lowering their hands, while holding their elbows near their sides." (Gifford 1927, 241).

☐ **Wormwood** is not a tree but a plant that appears in the spring and summer months primarily. In the Bear Dance, wormwood is used to "calm down bear and rattlesnake." Read Chapter Fifteen. It is worn behind the ear, hanging from one's belt, as well as held in one's hands. Wormwood is sometimes put in the nose as a sinus medicament.

☐ The **wososa** consisted of a stick whereon was tied many dried cocoons, each filled with acorns and grass-seeds. "The rattle could be heard to fall as the ghost departed." (Kroeber 1929, 272).

☐ **Dream story** is patterned from story line in "Sison" provided in Uldall and Shipley (1966, 25-29).

☐ **O-to,** the Seven Stars, are the Pleiades.

☐ **Panthers** probably represent the California mountain lion rather than California bobcats, which are smaller.

Chapter Six

☐ *Tuj-ma Ole Jamin* literally is "Coyote Sleeping Place Mountain" for what is today **Mt. Diablo.** This name is author-developed and linguistically created.

☐ **Esto-Yamani** literally means "middle-mountain" or "mountain set in the center." Today it is commonly known as the **Sutter Buttes.**

That "Aikat stood upon its highest peak and made camp" is referenced by Richard Simpson (1977, 28). His Indian informant was Liz Enos.

"Respected that the dead went to the Buttes to linger four days," as stated by Maidu informant Amanda Wilson upon stating this to Ermine W. Voegeline (1942, 119-341).

"These ghosts strayed around and blew about crying constantly," taken from Francis A. Riddell (1978, 382).

The Buttes and the flat country around them were unowned (Kroeber 1932, 268).

Account of seeing the "lights from fires of spirit campers" by informant Bud Bain as recorded by Dorothy Hill, circa 1972. Locals say that in the Pass Road area to the south of the Buttes natural gas seeps exist, and that in combination with certain atmospheric conditions the "mysterious light" phenomenon may partly be accounted for.

South Butte stands the tallest, 2,132 feet above sea level.

☐ **Pe,** pronounced pay.

☐ **Grasshopper preparation** method taken from Norman Wilson (1972, 36).

☐ **Molokúm** means "Morning Star Dance-House."

☐ All Secret Society ceremonies held inside the dance house only permitted men inside. Women who were menstruating could never **enter a dance house.** Also, only men could enter a ceremonial sweathouse.

☐ Maidu were known to say that their **dead went to the Marysville Buttes.** (Kroeber 1932, 272).

☐ The **language transition** zone was roughly midway between the Bear and Yuba Rivers.

☐ In legend times, **feather mantles** were also edged with acorns and pine nuts.

☐ In the Valley Nisenan, *Akit Aikat,* their **greatest dance,** Biller Preacher states that the *moki* dress in the dance house. They traditionally do not enter from outdoors (Kroeber 1932, 384). The *aki* was the main ceremonial dance of the Hill Northwestern Maidu, and like the *hesi* of the Patwin and Sacramento Maidu, was performed in the fall and spring. (Loeb 1932-34, 170).

☐ **Bullroarers** in the Chico Maidu area were used simply as toys. They were used in initiation ceremonies, however, within the western half of the Ku'ksū cult area of California (Loeb 1932, 193, 227).

☐ Medicine had been purposely blown on all head feathers and cloaks by the doctors so only dancers may touch them. The doctors give the **dancers medicine** to chew so the feathers won't injure them.

Only old, experienced dancers may don dance regalia without using medicine. The head dancer at Auburn had a root which he passed four times about his head.

He then chewed it. Sugar-pine pitch properly "fixed" served the purpose also (Beals 1933, 398-399.)

☐ Because it brought "bad luck," the **eagle was never shot.** (Dixon 1905, 192-195).

☐ Recall in the creation story that "... Coyote reached the mountain **sweathouse and the door** was on the *west*" (italics mine). However, Norman Wilson's excavations of Sacramento Valley sites found main doors at the east side at two sites, one of which was Sac-29.

☐ Another barrier to ascertaining what the sacred entrance looked like is the fact that the Indians held the belief or "superstition" that bad luck followed the **divulgence of tribal lore** to white men or to any outsiders (Dillon 1967, 91).

☐ That **spiritual power** called *pe...* is free floating, lays about and is obtainable, is taken from John Lowell Bean (1975, 58, 62).

Chapter Seven

☐ There were primarily **two kinds of doctors:** curing or sucking doctors and dream doctors. Old-Grouse Woman in the story is a hybrid of these two.

☐ **Sources for procuring medicines** (Duncan 1961, 6; Rathbun, *Destruction of,* 1973, 14-15).

☐ A doctor used **special feathers** to determine whether or not a patient was following directions. The feather's color would change at the tip, from black to white or white to black. Also the shape at the end of the feather might change where the two contrasting colors met, if a person was sick or was not following the doctor's directions (Gardner 1977, 63-64).

☐ **Sila** arrows (Beals 1933, 401; Kroeber 1929, 274; Loeb 1932-34, 163).

☐ Poison **halky** (Duncan 1961, 14).

☐ Children told to **"make water"** over bush. (Beals 1933, 387).

☐ **So poisonous that you will kill** anyone you touch (Beals 1933, 386).

☐ **Doctor's** *dokdok* **bag** (Gayton 1925, *Bancroft Library notes*).

☐ **Tobacco** *(Nicotiana attenuata)* was the only cultivated plant.

☐ California Indians believe we are in the **fourth world** and that after the next destruction there will be a fifth world.

☐ Prior to the visit of that awful scourge among the Maidu, the **small pox** in 1852, one Indian prophesized that "bad spirits" were about them and that before long a great many Indians would die. Small pox came shortly thereafter killing thousands in the counties, thus confirming their superstition. (Hurtado 1976, 116).

Chapter Eight

☐ Chiefs and special hunters with **two or more wives** is discussed in Uldall and Shipley (1966, 135) and Beals (1933, 373).

Mother-in-law and father-**in-law taboos** are discussed by Leob (1932-1934, 177)

☐ **Marriage consummation** is discussed in Beals (1933, 371).

☐ Tea of mistletoe to make the **delivery prompt** is taken from Merriam (1966, 310).

☐ Reasons for restraining a baby is taken in part from Margolin (1981, 11-12).

☐ **"Nopanny"** was Bidwell's first wife and lived at *Mikahopdo,* says Brian Bibby.

Chapter Nine

☐ Dead who **"look back"** (Uldall and Shipley 1966, 87).

Nisenan informant Bill Joe told me that he had once met a deer which he was somehow unable to shoot although he had a rifle with him. He took my suggestion that it might have been his mother. It was with relief that he learned I too might believe in this transformation and therefore could understand his feelings.

☐ **Creator's words:** six paragraphs about Coyote beginning with "Good is the wisdom..." have been adopted from Richard Simpson's 1971 book, *Ooti: A Maidu Legacy,* pp. 23-24, by permission of the author and of the publisher, Celestial Arts in Berkeley, California.

☐ **Coyote's arrows** have but two feathers (Uldall and Shipley 1966, 20).

Chapter Ten

☐ **Chucumnes** were the Nisenan's bitter enemies (Lienhard 1939).

☐ **Torture** is discussed in Loeb (1932-34, 144-145). Story of woman being tied to tree and having her hands and feet burnt off is taken from Loeb (p. 176).

☐ The number of arrows indicated the number of **days to elapse before the attack** is taken from Faye (1923, 43), as is fact that a line was drawn between the two camps.

☐ **Children being made to return the arrows** to their parent in battle is taken from R. Rathburn, *The Destruction of the People* (1973, 103).

☐ The "victor" would have to **pay the highest price** is taken from Loeb (1932-34, 176).

☐ **Armor** is discussed in R. Rathbun, *The Destruction of the People* (1973, 79) mainly used in northern Sacramento Valley, Siskiyou and Northern Maidu areas.

☐ **Rattlesnake poison** is taken from Uldall and Shipley (1966, 75).

☐ *Hudessi* or **"brave man" killer** dodging arrows is taken from R. Rathbun, *The Destruction of the People* (1973, 29).

☐ **Women danced during the war** is taken from R. Rathbun also, *ibid,* p. 71.

☐ **"Finish-up" fellows** is taken from Uldall and Shipley (1966, 99).

☐ **Taboos about those who have killed** someone is taken from R. Rathbun, *The Destruction of the World* (1973, 82).

☐ **Wa-pum-ni** under Chief Tucollie today is the Latrobe, Califorina area.

☐ A **"marked" grove of trees** *(topeca)* meant that the owners had cleared off a bare spot on the ground by the trees and left dried acorn there as a sign for passers-by (Uldall and Shipley 1966, 97-98).

☐ This **battle field site** has since been washed away by mining operations (Beals 1933, 367).

☐ Besides eagle feathers, sometimes chicken hawk feathers were reserved for **"war" arrows.**

☐ Just **one bow shot apart** for combat would be about 100 yards apart. See Loeb 1932-1934, 176.

☐ Some *Tahñ*-kum (Oroville) men had come to **Oregon Creek** (5 miles north of North San Juan on Hwy 49) and captured one *Chucumnes* woman and two men.

Chapter Eleven

☐ The **white goose,** referred to as "God's bird," is referenced in Powers (1877, 310). *O'lele*, the white luck bird is cited in Kroeber (1929, 275).

☐ Matos' concern "why do the **strangers have no wives** nor children with them" is partly adapted from Margolin (1981, 15).

☐ During the Modoc War of 1877, Curly-headed Doctor "took a **long cord and painted it red...**" (Pay 1963, 67).

☐ **Gabriel Moraga's** location on October 9, 1808, involving skirmish is not certain. It may well have been along another river. The diary sections used are all taken from a secondary source, namely, Cutter (1957, 13-25). The primary source diary is in the Bancroft Library at Univ. of Calif., Berkeley, among the Cowan papers (referred to as the Huntington Collection).

☐ Although **the league** was not a standard measurement, but varied from place to place and from person to person, Moraga's league was approximately the average league, roughly 2.75 miles.

☐ Indians discovered along the Cosumnes River were probably **Ko-ni or Plains Miwok.**

☐ One **vara** equals 33 inches.

☐ The sharp object which the Indians threw at Moraga's soldier and struck him on October 9th was probably a **spear,** not an atlatl.

☐ Moraga noted in his diary that he had found eleven **Indian villages** on the *Llagas* (American River), seven on the Sacramento (Feather River), and three on the Jesus Maria (Sacramento River). See McGowen (1961, 18).

☐ Moraga's Indian **interpreter** was probably Wintun.

☐ Moraga and his soldiers probably **ascended the Sacramento River** as far as present day Butte City, or perhaps slightly farther.

☐ Where Tawec speaks out against the **white man's religion,** part of his speech is adapted from Nancy Wood, *Many Winters* (Garden City, NJ: Doubleday & Company, 1974), p. 46.

☐ **Non-Indian trappers** along the American River between 1808 and 1828 would probably be Americans. Canadians with the Hudson Bay Company did not get established in Vancouver until 1829. Starting in 1830 until 1844, brigades of the Hudson's Bay Company visited the Sacramento Valley every year. (McGowen 1961, 22).

☐ Yototowi is actually the Nisenan name for the **first woman** in their creation story, while Morning-Star Woman is the name of the first woman in the Northwest Maidu creation story.

☐ There were a number of **"Non-Indian" Expeditions** that reached into Maidu-Nisenan territory that could have led to "rumors" about light-skinned strangers:

In 1817 Padre Narcisco Duran of the Mission San Jose, accompanied by Don Luis Arguello for protection, sailed as far as the *rancheria* of the *Chucumnes*; a number of women and infants were baptized (Sutter 1936, 42).

In 1821 Luis Arguello took a large expedition up the west side of the Valley whereby he encountered hostilities with the Indians along the Sacramento River (five Indians killed). He named the Feather River, *Rio de las Plumas* because of the great number of feathers from water fowl he saw on the stream (McGowan 1961, 20-21).

In 1823 Otto van Kotzebue, a German in the Russian Imperial Navy accounts he sailed well up the Sacramento River perhaps as far as the American.

Also Hudson Bay Company expeditions after Jedediah Smith included Alexander McLeod (1828-29), Skene Ogden (1829-30), and John Work (1832-33). Theory has it that Work's party that traded for beaver with the central Valley Indians brought in what many think was malaria.

☐ **Jedediah Smith story.** Precise locations today where events occurred back in 1828 are hindered by the fact that the American River was "realigned about 1868" (McGowan 1961, 21).

☐ **"Two Indians Killed"** is taken from Jedediah Strong Smith, *The Southwest Expedition of Jedediah Smith: His Personal Account of the Journey to California, 1826-1827.* 1977, pp. 154-157, A.H. Clark Co., Glendale, California

☐ **"Another Indian Killed, One-Wounded"** and "10 Year Old Girl Scared to Death" come from Sullivan (1936, 158-159).

☐ Not all of **Smith's party** were Caucasians. Peter Rand was a black and former slave.

☐ Jedediah Smith may have been using the name **"Rio Ojotska"** before, possibly the Russian name for this river. In May of 1833, Captain John R. Cooper, when seeking a tract of land along this river from Governor Figuero, used the name "Rio Ojotska" in his petitioned document and on "... his accompanying map, indicating that Russians from Fort Ross were also probably in the valley by that time. The word *Ojotska* seems to have been a phonetic spelling for *Okhatsakaia* meaning "hunter" (McGowan 1961, 22).

☐ The chronology for "historic" **names for the American River** is: 1808, *"Rio de las Llagas"* (River of Sorrows) as named by Ensign Gabriel Moraga in honor of Christ's suffering on the cross; 1828, the "Wild River" by Jedediah Smith in commemoration of the singular wildness "of these Indians and the novel occurances that made it appear so forcibly"; 1837, *"Rio de los Americanos"* by Governor Alvarado who called it such because the area was frequented by American "trappers of revolutionary proclivities." (Erwin G. Gudde, 1966, *California Place Names.* 3rd edition, p. 9. UC Press, Berkeley.

Chapter Twelve

☐ Fully **20,000 people died in 1833** in the Great Central Valley (Cook 1943, 30-37).

☐ **Enfanticide** practiced when mother died (Powers (1877, 328).

☐ **Killings in the Pitchiku dance house** area occurred in the 1820's (outside Roseville). Nevada City people massacred many during a Big Time at Rockland. Because many people from other places were present, Nevada City people became widely disliked and mistrusted. One fight arose from a brawl at Nevada City during a mourning ceremony, in which a man got killed. Others attributed the fighting due to Nevada City people stealing salt near Rockland.

Two Nevada City Indians once shot several people, through the smokehole atop the dance house, during a Big Time at Iowa Hill. One was captured but denied complicity. He was offered his freedom if he told his accomplice's name. He did so and he was promptly shot. The other man was ambushed several weeks later (Beals 1933, 366).

☐ **Opuley** (ahp-ou-lay) was the name of the Auburn Indian village.

☐ "Those hill doctors sent **bad air** into the Valley to avenge those killings." (Pay 1963, 23 and Wilson 1957)

☐ "They had **'caught' the thing** that was causing the sickness and they were going to drown it." Taken from Helen H. Roberts, *Concow-Maidu Indians of Round Valley–1926*, as edited by Dorothy J. Hill, pp. 7-8.

☐ Plaster acorn **dough "marks"** to prevent bad luck is also taken from Helen Roberts, *ibid*, pp. 2-4.

☐ The **World Renewal** celebration was held in the spring season when plants were growing again, hence, the start of a new year and time for prayers. Today, the **Bear Dance** conducted in Janesville (see Chapter 15) has seemingly included some of these aspects.

☐ By 1910, the **Nisenan and Maidu declined to 1,100,** including those of mixed bloods. "Last Konkow Maidu Indian Dies in Yuba," *Sacramento Bee* (October 17, 1970), p. All, c. 1-2.

☐ The "**killings** of Opuley (Auburn) and Hó-man (Nevada City) men."

Chapter Thirteen

☐ **John Augustus Suter** (American spelling is Sutter) was born in 1803 near Basle, Switzerland of Swiss parents. For his first fifteen years, he lived in Kandern, Baden, Germany. At age 16, he went to work in Basel, Switzerland. He soldiered in the Berne, Switzerland infantry reserve where his highest rank was "first lieutenant." Bankrupt and wanted by creditors, Sutter left his wife and four children, arriving in New York in 1834. By 1836, Sutter was in Santa Fe. From Kansas City, the Oregon Trail, Fort Vancouver, the Sandwich Islands, Sitka, Alaska, and finally, Yerba Buena (later San Francisco), he focused on the interior of Alta California to try to lay claim to empire. Joseph McGowan asserts that Sutter set foot on what is today Sacramento on August 15, 1839 (1961, 25). He landed along the south side of the American River 200 feet north of the official bronze monument at 29th and B Streets. Precisely when Sutter commenced building the fort is controversy. While McGowan says 1841, California State Archaeologist John Kelly says 1840. The fort took four years to build. Sutter moved with his visiting family to Hock Farm in 1850. He left Sacramento for good in 1865. He died in 1880 in Washington, D.C.

☐ Originally, Sutter brought ten **Hawaiians** with him (eight men and two women). The names of eight are fairly well agreed upon, namely: (1.) Kanaka Harry who was put in charge of the Hock Farm; (2.) Maintop, who commanded Sutter's launch; (3.) Manuiki (Manaiki), Harry's wife, for whom Sutter had the dearest affections; (4.) Harry's brother-in-law, who confusingly, was known by the same name as his sister, Manuiki; (5.) Harry's brother (no name) who served Sutter until he drowned in Suisun Bay in 1847; (6.) Ioanne Keaala o Kaaina (called John Kelly by the Americans) who married Su-mai-neh, a Konkow elder and artist; (7.) Sam Kapu, and (8.) Elena, wife of Sam Kapu. The later two subsequently had one son, John Kapu, who married Paméla Cleanso, sister of Captain "Mike" Cleanso, the last Nisenan chief at *Kadema* (near present Watt Avenue bridge) whose son was "Blind" Tom. Sources include McGowan (1961, 24—45), Dillon (1967, 97), Sutter (1939, *vii*).

☐ **Chief Anashe's Walagumnes** presumably spoke Plains Miwok. This first encounter took place twelve miles south from the mouth of the American,

☐ A **pinnace** is a four-oared boat, usually kept aboard a larger ship; used in ferrying people around harbors.

☐ **Sutter's Fort** rests atop an Indian village site, but records give no indication which Indian groups(s) occupied it.

☐ Sutter blasted his **"brass thunder tubes"** nine times. Dillon (1967, 89).

☐ Indians **eating horse meat** shared by Norman Wilson. Also cited in Ricketts (1978, 23).

☐ **Bulldog** was later killed by a grizzly. The dog's name is unknown.

☐ **Sutter's quote** "In the spring of 1840..." from Severson (1973).

☐ Heinrich Lienhard refers to the **Pusuni village** as the "Bushumne tribe." Sutter told him about the animosity between the Indian groups (Nisenan versus *Chucumne* [Miwok]) Statement that the "Bushumne tribe... subsequently proved to be Sutter's most capable workers" is taken from Lienhard (1939, 7).

☐ Sutter fed the Indians in **long narrow troughs** (Uldall and Shipley 1966, 67; and Peterson 1985, 26).

☐ Fort Sutter **Indian bodyguard soldiers** comes from McGowan (1961, 30) and personal conversations with George Stammerjohan of California's Dept. of Parks and Recreation.

☐ Sutter's 1840 **rescue of Indian girl captives** taken from Uldall and Shipley (1966, 69) and Dillon (1967, 105).

☐ References to **"slaving Indians"** taken from Dillion (1967, 199); also Peterson article (1985).

☐ **Manuiki dearest** to Sutter, Dillon (1967, 94–95).

☐ **Chief Raphero** story from Dillon (1967, 198).

☐ **Gold amounts** extracted by Indians taken from J.O. Sherwood, letter of November 14, 1851. See notes by Ricketts (1978).

☐ **Fall 1848 massacre** of twenty-five Indians along Bear River, the retalitory raids by Indians at Spanish Bar, including William Daylor's account taken from article without writer's name, "White Man's Vengeance," *Sacramento Bee,* (Sept. 6, 1949), p. A19. Reference is made that editor Edward Kemble, who published the *Placer Times* inside the Fort first on April 28, 1849, was unable to get much reliable information. Accounts also cited in Ricketts (1978, 18–19) and Rawls (1976, 38–40).

☐ **Round Valley story** taken from Rathbun, *Destruction of The People* (1973, 54); Hill (1970, 77). Maidu's called Round Valley "Standing Quiet," from Charles W. Kenn, "Descendants of Captain Sutter's *Kanakas,*" a paper read at San Jose by Sacramento Indian Museum Docent Henry Collins, p. 93. Said paper is in author's files. Marie Potts information from narration of movie "Chen-Kut-Pam" (Little Sharp Eyes).

Chapter Fourteen

☐ **The beginning 1903 narrative** is taken from C.H. Merriam (1966), and "Blind" Tom Cleanso recollections have been pieced together from Shipley and Uldall (1966), E.W. Gifford (1927), A.L. Kroeber and D. Forde (1929), E.M. Loeb (1933), plus data about the *Kadema* site (Sac-192/196) by John S. Clemmer from the Archaeological Laboratory of California Dept. of Parks and Recreation.

☐ **Nisenan vocabulary** from Gayton (1925), Nisenan Notebook No. 1, p. 32, 120 (Bancroft Library in Berkeley).

☐ **The name Cleanso,** (Klinso), comes from Grimšo, Grimshaw (Shipley and Uldall 1966, 174).

☐ Most likely **the girl who took Merriam over** to the Broderick side was Lillie Williams (1881-1961), daughter of Pamēla Cleanso who had married Hawaiian John Kapu. Lillie Williams and "Blind" Tom were cousins. Lillie Williams was born at *Pusuni;* was survived at her death by one brother, James Adams, and many descendants. "Lillie Williams of Nisenan Indian Tribe Dies At 80," *Sacramento Bee,* (August 24, 1961), p. C3.

☐ **Tom married a mulatto** from Canada—Lizzie Terry. They had no children. (Gayton 1925).

☐ Tom stayed at the State Industrial **Home for the Blind** in Oakland, California.

☐ Fact that Dolores, the mother, came from **Yukulme** comes from John S. Clemmer Papers.

☐ Text of the **"The Cleanso Family"** by Uldall and Shipley has discrepancy by stating "His elder sister . . . is buried at *Kadema.* He buried his elder sister at *Pusune.* Page 175.

☐ Upon completion of digging at CA-Sac-192/196 by John S. Clemmer, **burials of the Cleanso and Cook families were reinterred** to East Lawn Memorial Cemetery on June 11, 1960. Reinternment of Mike Cleanso, and Dolores and Ida Cleanso were completed. Also, John K. Cook, Hawaiian-Indian, and Lillian Cook were reinterred. Records read "These are five bone boxes of the Cook and Cleanso families. They are all placed in one grave and one christy vault." The burial location is Section D, Row 5, Grave 3A. On the bronze grave marker Dolores is listed after Capt. Mike's name, then Ida. Ida is possibly Mike's first wife, since Dolores is much younger than Mike in the photograph (page 175), and chiefs were allowed two or more wives. On cemetery records, Mike Cleanso's race is stated as Hawaiian-Indian which must be a mistake, for Mike Cleanso died in 1901, but he lived to be just over 100 years old which predates the arrival of Sutter's *Kanakas*. The next of kin for the burials was Lillie Williams. She is identified as informant.

☐ **Year of "Blind" Tom's death,** circa 1932, based on catalog numbers 1968-98-1, a.-d., at San Diego Museum of Man reads "4 abalone shell ornaments overlooked when Blind Tommy (a Nisenan Maidu) was buried. Found in the ruins of his cabin (1932);" as stated in letter to Richard Burrill from Craig D. Bates, Curator of Ethnography, Yosemite National Park. Typed page, however, among papers by John S. Clemmer reads " 'Blind' Tom stayed alone at *Kadema* until about 1938, when he became too old and feeble to stay alone." Archaeology Laboratory, California Department of Parks and Recreation.

☐ Use of names of **Big Meadows, Matos, and So-se-yah-mah** are all fictionally embellished characters in this chapter. Hunchup is the name of a former Maidu medicine man, however.

☐ Merriam cites a **former name** for Sac-192/196. "About nine miles easterly from Sacramento City is the old Spanish-American 'Rancho del Rio Americano,' now known by two names—**Horse Ranch and Hop Ranch.**" Area circa 1960 was called Shelby's Stables and Whittenbrook Ranch. Formerly, Merriam states, it was the site of Pä'-we-nan *rancheria Hah-kon.* (Merriam 1966, 62; Bennyhoff 1961, 253; Kroeber 1929, 254).

☐ Merriam writes that **"Blind" Tom was born at Poo-soó-ne** *(Pusuni)*; Kroeber, on the other hand, understood that Tom's father was born at *Pusuni* and Tom himself at *Kadema.*

☐ Many of the **Nisenan descendents** are now members of the *rancheria* at Shingle Springs, California.

☐ Apparently **Paméla moved from Broderick** to *Kadema,* for Uldall and Shipley conclude to say after Tom Cleanso had died, "The Indians at *Pusuni* and *Kadema* are gone now, the many Indians there are gone. Paméla is the only one living there. That is that." (Uldall and Shipley, 1966, 175).

Epilogue

☐ **Physical descriptions of the Buttes** are taken partly from the following: Peter Michael Jensen, *Prehistoric Settlement Pattern of Peace Valley in the Sutter Buttes* (Davis, California, unpublished master's thesis, 1969) and "Notes on the Archaeology of the Sutter Buttes, California," *Papers on California and Great Basin Prehistory,*" No. 2 by the Center for Archaeological Research at Davis, 1970), pp. 45, 48-49. (Citied in Jensen's report were Heizer and Baumhoff 1962, 237.)

Ted Rieger, "Hiking the Sutter Buttes," *Sacramento Union,* December 6, 1984, pp. D1 and D3.

Bibliography

Beals, Ralph L. 1933. "Ethnology of the Nisenan." *University of California Publications in American Archaeology and Ethnology.* Vol. 31, No. 6.

Bean, John Lowell. 1975. "Power And Its Applications in Native California," *Journal of California Anthropology.* Vol. 2, No. 1.

Bennyhoff, James. 1961. *Ethnogeography of the Plains Miwok.* Berkeley, PhD. thesis.

Chase, Don M. *People of the Valley: The Concow Maidu.* Sebastopol, California.

Clemmer, John S. (Sac-192/196) Letters on file with Archaeological Laboratory. California Department of Parks and Recreation.

Cook, Sherburne F. 1943. *The Conflict Between the California and White Civilization.* II Ibero-Americana 22, Berkeley.

_____. 1976. *Populations of the California Indians 1769-1970.* UC Press, Berkeley.

Cutter, Donald C. translator and editor. 1957. *The Diary of Ensign Gabriel Moraga's Expedition of Discovery in the Sacramento Valley, 1808.* G. Dawson, Los Angeles.

Dillon, Richard. 1967. *Fool's Gold.* Coward-McCann, Inc., New York.

Dixon, Roland. 1902. "Maidu Myths." *American Museum of Natural History Bulletin.* Vol. 17, Part 2.

_____. 1905. "The Northern Maidu." *American Museum of Natural History Bulletin.* Vol. 17, Part 5.

Duncan III, John W. 1964. *Maidu Ethnobotany.* CSU Thesis, Sacramento.

Ellzasser, Albert and Heizer, F. 1980. *The Natural World of the California Indians.* UC Press, Berkeley.

Faye, Paul-Louis. 1923. "Notes on the Southern Maidu," *University of California Publications in American Archaeology and Ethnology,* Vol. 20, No.3.

Gardner, Ruth. 1977. *Life History of Lalook: Louis Kelly.* CSU Thesis, Sacramento.

Gayton, A.H. "Southern Nisenan Ethnographic Notes and Vocabularies," Document No. 120, University of California Archives. Cited in *Guide to Ethnological Documents* (1-203), compiled by Valory, Archaeological Research Facility. See Nisenan Notebook No.1 at Bancroft Library, Berkeley.

Gifford, Edward W. 1927. "Southern Maidu Religious Ceremonies." *American Anthropologist.* n.s. Vol. 29, No. 3.

Hendrix, Louise Butts. *Sutter Buttes: Land of Histum Yani.* Sutter County, California.

Hill, Dorothy, 1969. *Collection of Maidu Indian Folklore of Northern California.* Northern California Indian Association, Chico.

_____. 1970. *Indians of Chico Rancheria: An Ethnohistoric Survey.* CSU Thesis, Chico.

Hurtado, Albert Leon. 1976. *The Maidu and California Indian Policy.* CSU Thesis, Sacramento.

Jensen, Peter. 1970. "Notes on the Archaeology of the Sutter Buttes, California." *Papers on California and Great Basin Prehistory.* No. 2 by the Center for Archaeological Research, Davis, Calif.

_____. 1969. *Prehistoric Settlement Pattern of Peace Valley in The Sutter Buttes.* Thesis, Davis, Calif.

Jewell, Donald P. 1987. *Indians of the Feather River Tales and Legends of the Concow Maidu of California.* Ballena Press, Menlo Park, California.

Kroeber, A.L. 1929. "The Valley Nisenan." *University of California, Publications in American Archaeology and Ethnology.* Vol. 24, No. 4.

_____. 1932. "The Patwin and Their Neighbors." *University of California Publications in American Archaeology and Ethnology.* Vol. 29, No. 4.

Lienhard, Heinrich. 1941. *A Pioneer at Sutter's Fort 1846-1850.* Edited by Margaret E. Wilbur. Calafia Series, No. 3, Calafia Society, Los Angeles.

Lienhard, Heinrich. 1939. *I Knew Sutter.* CSU Sacramento Library.

Loeb, Edwin M. 1932-34. "The Eastern Kuksu Cult." *Univ. of California Publications in American Archaeology and Ethnology.* Vol. 33, No. 2.

Margolin, Malcolm. 1981. *The Way We Lived.* Heyday Books, Berkeley.

McGowen, Joseph A. 1961. *History of the Sacramento Valley.* Lewis Historical Publishing Company, New York.

Merriam, C. Hart. 1966. *Reports of the University of California Archaeological Survey,* No. 68. Part 1, edited by Robert F. Heizer.

Pay, Verne, 1963. *Primitive Pragmatists.* Univ. of Washington Press, Seattle.

Peterson, Richard H. 1985. "Sutter and the Indians," *The Californians.* March/April.

Powers, Stephen. 1877. "Tribes of California." *Contributions to North American Ethnology.* United States Geographical and Geological Survey of the Rocky Mountain Region. Department of the Interior.

Rathburn, Robert. 1973. *Destruction of the People.* Brother William Press, Berkeley.

_____. 1973. *Sun, Moon and Stars.* Brother William Press, Berkeley.

Rawls, James J. 1976. "Gold Diggers: Indian Miners in the California Gold Rush," *California Historical Quarterly.* Spring.

Ricketts, Norma Baldwin. 1978. *Historic Cosumnes and the Slough House Pioneer Cemetery.* Daughters of Utah Pioneers, Salt Lake City.

Riddell, Francis A. 1978. "Maidu and Koncow." *Handbook of North American Indians.* Vol. 8: California. Edited by Robert Heizer. Smithsonian Institution Press, Press, Washington, D.C.

Rieger, Ted. 1984, Dec. 6. "Hiking the Sutter Buttes." *Sacramento Union News.*

Severson, Thor. 1973. *Sacramento, An Illustrated History: 1839 to 1874.* California Historical Society.

Simpson, Richard. 1977. *Ooti: A Maidu Legacy.* Celestial Arts, Millbrae, California.

Smith, Jedediah Strong. *The Southwest Expedition of Jedediah Strong Smith: His Personal Account of the Journey to California, 1826-1827.* Published in 1977 by A.H. Clark Co., Glendale, Calif.

Sullivan, Maurice S. 1936. *Jedediah Smith, Trader and Trail Breaker.* New York Press, New York.

Sutter, John A. *Sutter's Own Story.* Published in 1936 by G.P. Putnam Sons, New York.

Sutter, John A. *New Helvetia Diary.* Published in 1939 by The Society of California Pioneers/Grabhorn Press, San Francisco.

Uldall, Hans Jorgen and Shipley, William. 1966. *Nisenan Texts and Dictionary.* Univ. of California Press, Berkeley.

Voegeline, Ermine W. 1942. "Culture Element Distributions: Vol. XX Northwest California," *Anthropological Records,* Vol. 17.

Wilson, Norman L. 1972. "Notes of Foothill Nisenan Food Technology." in Eric W. Ritter's *Archaeological Investigations in the Auburn Reservoir Area.*

Wilson, Norman and Arlean Towne. 1979. *Selected Bibliography of Maidu Ethnography and Archaeology.* Dept. of Parks and Recreation, Sacramento, California.

Appendix A
Nisenan Grammar

Aikat—Creator

am-ty—women's game involving use of scoop-shaped seed-beater baskets

Banakam mo-lo kyle—Morning Star Woman

cá-win—poison

citapai o mie—take care of oneself and farewell

dokdok—doctor's bag

dul—great foot drum

halky—seed from a small plant, very poisonous

hudessi—special "brave man" champion

huk—headman

Kadema—(Ga-dem-a) village that was near present Watt Avenue bridge (see map page 15)

Ka'kimim kumi—spirit house

k-öi—war

Ku kini busdi—soul; spirit

ku'ksū—wood spirit; has one leg and one eye

Ku'ksū hesi—Secret Society dance

Ku'ksū—Secret Society; also Koncow name for the first man

kúm—(koam) house

Esto-Yamani—Sutter Buttes

Makki—chief's headdress consisting of straight stick worn at the back of the head and decorated with woodpecker and quail feather and bits of abalone shell.

moki—feathered cloak

mom—water

No'to-mom—American River

o'-ldo—marsh reed used for arrow shaft

o'lele—white "luck" bird

ooti—acorn

O-to—seven stars, the Pleiades

pahno—grizzly bear

pe—(pā) spiritual power
pul—knotted string used for marking days past
punkok—smokehole
po-kelma—feathered rope
rancherias—Spanish for Indian village
sila—doctor's "poison sticks" that can be hurled great distances
Ta'-doiko—half a mile east of Durham, California
temeya—initiate
tokas—bird bone whistle
Tuj-ma Ole Jamin—Mt. Diablo
Uk'o'yim-ni—I'm going. Good-bye.
Wadom buh-yee—Bear dance of the Mountain Maidu
wa-se—obsidian
wenne hon—"good feelings" or "good medicine"
wo le—white man
wö-o—Secret Society's crier
we-da—amulet
wolza—flicker feather headdress
wososo—cocoon rattle
wadada—elderberry clapper stick
yandih—Konkow Maidu word for "house" or "mountain"
Yĕ'poni—full initiate dancer
yok-koli—garland
yo-mi—medicine curing doctor

Appendix B

Indian Calendars

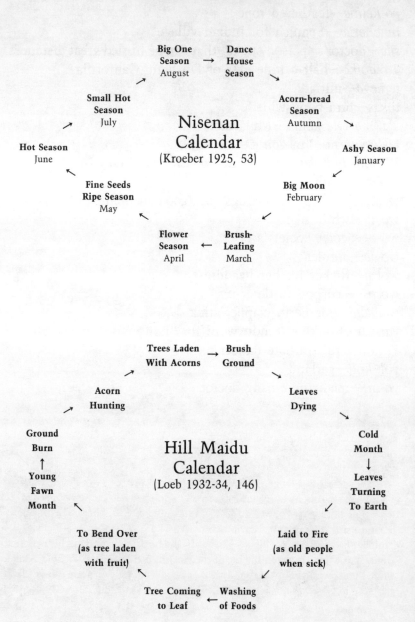

Big One
Season
August → Dance
House
Season

Small Hot
Season
July

Acorn-bread
Season
Autumn

Hot Season
June

Nisenan
Calendar
(Kroeber 1925, 53)

Ashy Season
January

Fine Seeds
Ripe Season
May

Big Moon
February

Flower
Season
April ← Brush-
Leafing
March

Trees Laden
With Acorns → Brush
Ground

Acorn
Hunting

Leaves
Dying

Ground
Burn
↑
Young
Fawn
Month

Hill Maidu
Calendar
(Loeb 1932-34, 146)

Cold
Month
↓
Leaves
Turning
To Earth

To Bend Over
(as tree laden
with fruit)

Laid to Fire
(as old people
when sick)

Tree Coming
to Leaf ← Washing
of Foods

Appendix C
The Search For Fire

At one time the people had found fire, and were going to use it; but Thunder (Wo'tomtomim maidum) wanted to take it away from them, as he desired to be the only one who should have fire. He thought that if he could do this, he would be able to kill all the people. After a time he succeeded, and carried the fire home with him, far to the south. He put Wo'swosim (a small bird) to guard the fire, and see that no one should steal it. Thunder thought that people would die after he had stolen their fire, for they would not be able to cook their food; but the people managed to get along. They ate most of their food raw, and sometimes got To'yeskom (another small bird) to look for a long time at a piece of meat; and as he had a red eye, this after a long time would cook the meat almost as well as a fire. Only the chiefs had their food cooked in this way.

All the people lived together in a big sweathouse. The house was as big as a mountain. Among the people was Lizard (Pi'tsaka) and his brother; and they were always the first in the morning to go outside and sun themselves on the roof of the sweathouse. One morning as they lay there sunning themselves, they looked west, toward the Coast Range, and saw smoke. They called to all the other people, saying that they had seen smoke far away to the west. The people, however, would not believe them; and Coyote came out, and threw a lot of dirt and dust over the two. One of the other people did not like this. He said to Coyote, "Why do you trouble people? Why don't you let others alone? Why don't you behave? You are always the first to start a quarrel. You always want to kill people without any reason." Then the other people felt sorry. They asked the two Lizards about what they had seen, and asked them to point out the smoke. The Lizards did so, and all could see the thin column rising up far to the west. One person said, "How shall we get that fire back? How shall we get it away from Thunder? He is a bad man. I don't know whether we had better try to get it or not." Then the chief said, "The best one among you had better try to get it. Even if Thunder is a bad man, we must try to get the fire. When we get there, I don't know how we shall get in; but the one who is the best, who thinks he can get in, let him try." Mouse, Deer, Dog, and Coyote were the ones who were to try, but all the other people went too. They took a flute with them, for they meant to put the fire in it.

They traveled a long time, and finally reached the place where the fire was. They were within a little distance of Thunder's house, when they all stopped to see what they would do. Wo'swosim, who was supposed to guard the fire in the house, began to sing, "I am the man who never sleeps. I am the man who never sleeps." Thunder had paid him for his work in beads, and he wore them about his neck and around his waist. He sat on the top of the sweathouse, by the smoke hole. After a while Mouse was sent up to try and see if he could get in. He crept up slowly till he got close to Wo'swosim, and then saw that his eyes were shut. He was asleep, in spite of the song that he sang. When Mouse saw that the watcher was asleep, he crawled to the opening and went in. Thunder had several daughters, and they were lying there asleep too. Mouse stole up quietly, and untied the waist-string of each one's apron, so that should the alarm be given, and they jump up, these aprons or skirts would fall off, and they would have to stop to fix them. This done, Mouse took the flute, filled it with fire, then crept out, and rejoined the other people who were waiting outside. Some of the fire was taken out and put in Dog's ear, the remainder in the flute being given to the swiftest runner to carry. Deer, however, took a little, which he carried on the hock of his leg, where today there is a reddish spot. For a while all went well, but when they were about halfway back, Thunder woke up, suspected that something was wrong, and asked, "What is the matter with my fire?" Then he jumped up with a roar of thunder, and his daughters were thus awakened, and also jumped up; but their aprons fell off as they did so, and they had to sit down again to put them on. After they were all ready, they went out with Thunder to give chase. They carried with them a heavy wind and a great rain and a hailstorm, so that they might put out any fire the people had. Thunder and his daughters hurried along, and soon caught up with the fugitives, and were about to catch them, when Skunk shot at Thunder and killed him. Then Skunk called out, "After this you must never try to follow and kill people. You must stay up in the sky, and be the thunder. That is what you will be." The daughters of Thunder did not follow any farther; so the people went on safely, and got home with their fire, and people have had it ever since.

(Dixon 1902, 65-67)

Appendix D
Hummingbird

One day Coyote was watching some hummingbirds darting about, and hanging apparently motionless in mid-air. He thought, "If I could only do that, all the girls in the country would fall in love with me." So he asked one of the hummingbirds, "How did you ever learn to do that? Teach me how to do it too, my cousin." Hummingbird replied, "The way that I learned to do it was to pick out a tall tree, climb up into it, and jump down; and just before hitting the ground I would say, '*Pinu'nu!*,' and that would turn me upwards again, and prevent my being hurt." Coyote was delighted, and went at once to find a suitable tree. He found one, climbed up, and leaped from the top; but before he could say "*Pinu'nu!*" he struck the ground and was killed. He lay there for a long time, till he was all dried up. Then two crows came along, and began to eat his eyes. Just at this time Coyote came to life again, and called out, "Did you think I was dead? I was only asleep, so leave me alone." Then he took a club and tried to hit the crows, but they flew away. As he lay there he looked about, and saw many large black crickets. He had been there so long that he was nearly starved, so he picked them up one by one, and ate them; but he did not seem to be able to appease his hunger. He ate and ate, but was just as hungry as before. He wondered to himself, "Why can't I fill up on them?" By and by he looked behind him, and found that he had lain there so long that there was a big hole in him, and the crickets were crawling out as fast as he swallowed them. When he saw this, he laughed and said, "Well, people can call me Coyote !"

(From Roland B. Dixon. "Maidu Myths," *American Museum of Natural History Bulletin.* 1902, Vol 17, Part 1, pp. 90-91.)

Appendix E

The To'lowim-Woman and the Butterfly-Man

A *To'lowim*-Woman went out to gather food. She had her child with her; and while she gathered food, she stuck the point of the cradleboard in the ground, and left the child thus alone. As she was busy, a large butterfly flew past. The woman said to the child, "You stay here while I go and catch the butterfly." She ran after it, and chased it for a long time. She would almost catch it, and then just miss it. She wore a deer-skin robe. She thought, "Perhaps the reason why I cannot catch the butterfly is because I have this on." So she threw it away. Still she could not catch the butterfly, and finally threw away her apron, and hurried on. She had forgotten all about her child, and kept on chasing the butterfly till night came. Then she lay down under a tree and went to sleep. When she awoke in the morning, she found a man lying beside her. He said, "You have followed me thus far, perhaps you would like to follow me always. If you would, you must pass through a lot of my people." All this time the child was where the woman had left it, and she had not thought of it at all. She got up, and followed the butterfly-man. By and by they came to a large valley, and the southern side was full of butterflies. When the two travelers reached the edge of the valley, the man said, "No one has ever got through this valley. People die before they get through. Don't lose sight of me. Follow me closely." They started, and traveled for a long time. The butterfly-man said, "Keep tight hold of me, don't let go." When they had got halfway through, other butterflies came flying about in great numbers. They flew every way, about their heads, and in their faces. They were fine fellows, and wanted to get the *To'lowim*-Woman for themselves. She saw them, watched them for a long time, and finally let go of her husband, and tried to seize one of these others. She missed him, and ran after him. There were thousands of others floating about; and she tried to seize, now one, now the other, but always failed, and so was lost in the valley. She said, "When people speak of the olden times by and by, people will say that this woman lost her husband, and tried to get others, but lost them, and went crazy and died." She went on then, and died before she got out of the valley. The butterfly-man she had lost went on, got through the valley, and came to his home.

(Dixon 1902, 95, 96)

Appendix F
The Rainbow

by Robert Rathbun

"The Rainbow—Coyote's Thingamajig
It moves so fast.
Women think it's the most beautiful
Thing in the world.
When they run after it
It slips away.
Coyote's rib—the Rainbow."

Coyote Man

(From *Sun, Moon and Stars*, Brother William Press, Berkeley. 1973.)

Appendix G
The Epidemic of 1833

"On our return in the summer of 1833 we found the valleys depopulated. From the head of the Sacramento to the great bend and slough of the San Joaquin we did not see more than six or eight Indians while large numbers of their skulls and dead bodies were to be seen under almost every shade tree near water, where uninhabited and deserted villages had been converted to graveyards."

J.J. Warner
(From *Gilbert, F.T. History of San Joaquin County, California.* 1879.)

A.S. Cook notes in "The Epidemic of 1830-1833 in California and Oregon,*" that the disaster spread from the north end of the Great Valley and theorized that it was malaria. He concludes:

"This is a startling and disturbing result. It means that fully 20,000 natives of the Great Central Valley died in 1833. It means that 3/4 of the Indians who had resisted 70 years of Spanish and Mexican domination were wiped out in one summer. It means that the red race in the heart of California was so crippled that it could offer but the shadow of opposition to the gold mining flood which swept over it in 1849."

(* *The University of California Publications in American Archaeology and Ethnology.* 1955.)

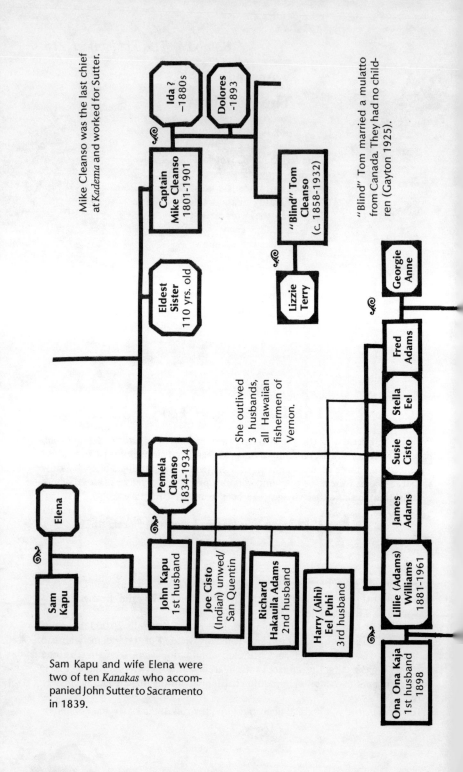

Mike Cleanso was the last chief at *Kadema* and worked for Sutter.

Ida ?
–1880s

Dolores
–1893

Captain
Mike Cleanso
1801-1901

"Blind" Tom
Cleanso
(c. 1858-1932)

Eldest
Sister
110 yrs. old

Lizzie
Terry

"Blind" Tom married a mulatto from Canada. They had no children (Gayton 1925).

Georgie
Anne

Fred
Adams

Stella
Eel

Peméla
Cleanso
1834-1934

She outlived 3 husbands, all Hawaiian fishermen of Vernon.

Susie
Cisto

James
Adams

Elena

John Kapu
1st husband

Joe Cisto
(Indian) unwed/
San Quentin

Richard
Hakauila Adams
2nd husband

Harry (Aihi)
Eel Puhi
3rd husband

Lillie (Adams)
Williams
1881-1961

Sam
Kapu

Sam Kapu and wife Elena were two of ten *Kanakas* who accompanied John Sutter to Sacramento in 1839.

Ona Ona Kaja
1st husband
1898

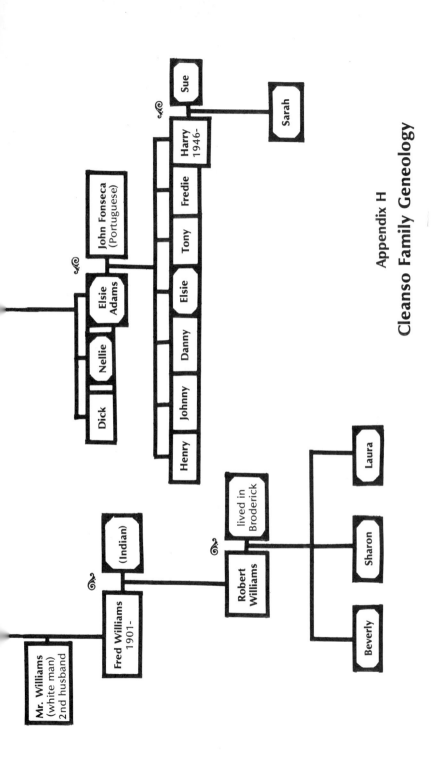

Appendix H

Cleanso Family Geneology

Appendix I
Asbill Family Geneology

Ioane Keaala o Kaaina (called John Kelly by the Americans) was one of ten *Kanakas* who accompanied John Sutter to Sacramento in 1839.

Frank discovered Round Valley on May 14, 1854.

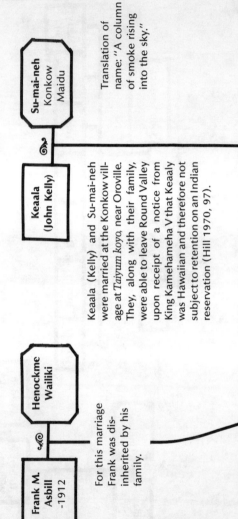

| Su-mai-neh | Keaala |
| Konkow Maidu | (John Kelly) |

Translation of name: "A column of smoke rising into the sky."

Keaala (Kelly) and Su-mai-neh were married at the Konkow village at *Taiyum koyo*, near Oroville. They, along with their family, were able to leave Round Valley upon receipt of a notice from King Kamehameha V that Keaaly was Hawaiian and therefore not subject to retention on an Indian reservation (Hill 1970, 97).

Frank M.	Henockme
Asbill	Wailiki
-1912	

For this marriage Frank was dis-inherited by his family.

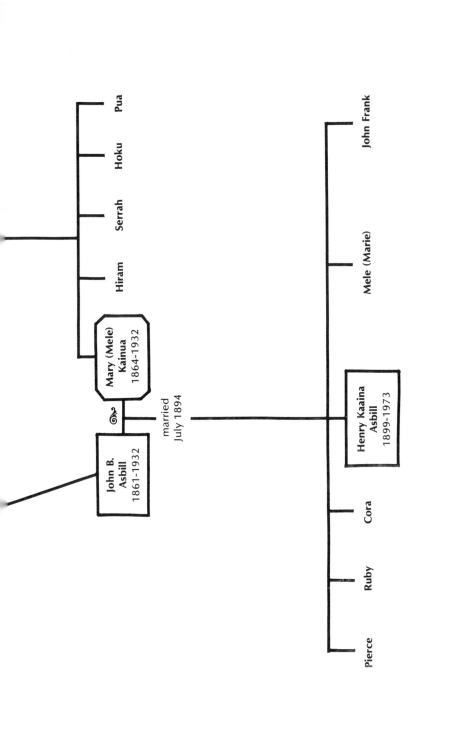